Taming the Beast

FREEING THE BEAST

TINA DONAHUE

Freeing the Beast
ISBN # 978-1-83943-801-1
©Copyright Tina Donahue 2017
Cover Art by Posh Gosh ©Copyright October 2017
Interior text design by Claire Siemaszkiewicz
Totally Bound Publishing

Published in 2019 by Totally Bound Publishing, United Kingdom.

Totally Bound Publishing books by Tina Donahue

Taming the Beast
Freeing the Beast
Surrendering to the Beast
Mastering the Beast
Muzzling the Beast
Disciplining the Beast
Seducing the Beast

FREEING
THE BEAST

Dedication

To Desiree Holt for introducing me to Rebecca,
my awesome editor. Ladies, you rock!

Chapter One

Ingredients for potions, along with books containing ancient and contemporary spells, littered Becca Salt's desk at From Crud to Stud, her New Orleans makeover service for supernatural beings.

She'd worked feverishly these last years, putting in the hours and expending the proverbial blood, sweat and tears to grow her company. When it came to management, hiring, promotion or a vision for the future, she had no equal.

As far as magic and attracting guys went, she was a total freaking dud. Love, it seemed, would never come her way. Conjuring, neither.

"Dammit, you can do this." She was a smart woman, able to rack up a perfect score on the SAT without cracking one textbook, which she'd hated, or cheating with sorcery. Witchcraft should have been a breeze.

If only she could concentrate on this stuff.

Designated Survivor played on her computer screen. Poor Kiefer Sutherland was in a hell of a mess trying to keep the country together while also dodging bullets, conspiracies and backstabbing lawmakers. Her addiction to this show, plus *Superstore*, *The Blacklist*, *Blindspot* and *The Good Fight* was her downfall. She also sensed being half witch and half mortal had something to do with her difficulty in mastering her craft. If her dad had been a warlock rather than a Democrat and a Teamster, she might have been into this stuff.

Her mom, Rowena, a crackerjack witch from an esteemed coven, hadn't agreed. "Study more and you'll do fine," she'd told Becca the other day. "This stuff's easier than what you had to do in high school."

She begged to differ. Dodging the mean girls, being invisible to the guys, navigating each horribly long day without a clique to protect her and looking as she did had been brutal. She wasn't a ghoul by any means, but she had boobs, hips and thighs like a normal person rather than a high-fashion model.

Countless diets later, here she was, nowhere close to a size zero and desperately wanting a Meat Lover's pizza chased by a Dove Bar.

Her stomach growled. Frustrated but determined, she waited until the commercial break and tried a simple trick—jerking her finger to open the age-old spells book.

The volume spun, flew across the room and landed on her needlepoint sofa.

"Crap." She paged through a witchcraft primer the old-fashioned way, like people had to do with print books before e-Readers had come around. Even though Google was supposed to contain all the information in the universe, including how to construct bombs, neither black nor white magic was included in its repertoire.

She rifled faster, her only option. The publication lacked an index and wasn't organized in any logical manner that she could determine. *Whoever put this thing together should be strangled.* A page tore. If she'd been at the top of her game, she would have repaired it by wiggling her nose as Samantha Stephens had done in that old TV show *Bewitched.* More than once, Becca had wondered why even the best witch would bother invoking powers to get material stuff. Next-day Amazon service, delivery drones and credit cards had made these skills unnecessary.

The commercial break ended. Kiefer was back, looking freaked out by the latest disaster but still presidential. She'd reached a page with instructions on how to change channels on a TV or cable programs on a laptop without using a remote, keystrokes or a mouse. At last, something she could use. Before she read details, she checked the copyright date. This baby had been written in the early nineteen-fifties but had regular updates. The last one had happened in the mid nineteen-eighties.

Sorcerers had to get with the times or they'd become as obsolete as looking stuff up rather than asking Siri for data, like a civilized person should.

After scanning the details for changing a show on a computer, she waited until the *Designated Survivor* credits scrolled down the screen. "Here goes." She held her breath, religiously repeated the words she needed and moved her finger in a tight circle as indicated in the graphic.

Her laptop shut off, powered back on and opened on a page for an advertisement selling potions at a discount. Even for a witch, there was no relief from pop-up ads.

Footfalls sounded in the hall and rushed toward her office.

Just what she didn't need, a staff member seeing her struggle with this stuff. Already her screw-ups with magic were legendary. Thankfully, she could count on her mom's assistance those few times someone needed conjuring that worked. Witchcraft was old-fashioned compared to moonlight therapy for weres, behavioral and aversion treatments for vamps, personality and charm courses for zombies. Nothing but the latest innovations for her clients.

With little time to hide these things the normal way, Becca muttered the words to make junk disappear and waved her hands for good measure.

Several books disintegrated, leaving paper dust in their wake. Others landed in her desk drawers. She could live with that. The potion ingredients settled behind her potted plants. From certain angles they were, indeed, invisible. She burst with pride. After some tweaking on the words and hand gestures, she'd have this spell down pat. Only a zillion others to go.

"Yo." Zoe stormed inside. "He's still not here."

Becca pulled up Excel on her laptop. "Who isn't?"

"Our client," Zoe fumed, looking like a waif from Hell, which she basically was. As a former human turned demon who'd crossed back to the lighter, mortal side, she'd taken to dressing like a Catholic schoolgirl. She wore a green plaid skirt that landed mid-calf, anklet socks, saddle shoes and a long-sleeved white blouse with a Peter Pan collar—a sweet, wholesome image except for her facial piercings. Four studs decorated her lower lip, two graced the bridge across her nose, a ring hung through one nostril and several adorned her dark eyebrows. The metal on her face glinted in the glow from streetlights that streamed through the windows. "The photographer's waited ten minutes already."

Ah, now Becca understood. He was here to shoot a demon's 'after' pictures to advertise the service for male shifters, genies, reapers, demons — and otherworldly beings. Every night, the staff whipped those poor slobs into shape so they could suppress their worst otherworldly natures, along with the problems that created, and present to mortal women as hotter-than-hell guys. For the most part.

Restraining all that evil and supernatural power wasn't easy.

Not even for a trooper like poor Zoe, one of Becca's BFFs and the best enforcer the service had ever had. If customers got too frisky or refused to do as the other staffers asked, Zoe got on their case and made them obey. Right now, irritation smoldered in her black eyes where sparks built from pinpoints to two wiggling flames. The red-orange color was seriously at odds with her pale skin and demure outfit.

Before Zoe had a literal meltdown, Becca talked fast. "Do we know where he lives?"

Once she had the client's location, she could send another customer to haul him in. Preferably a zombie. Those guys could give an IRS agent a run for his money. No matter what obstacles zombies faced, they kept coming and coming and coming. Not unlike the Energizer Bunny.

"He gave us an address not too far from here." Zoe cleared the gravel from her throat that made her sound like the centuries-old demon she was. She crossed her skinny arms over her chest, possibly to control her unruly emotions. Didn't work. Smoke rose from her long raven hair and shoulders and gave off a nasty sulfur stench. "I've called his cell phone twelve times. It keeps going to voice mail." She huffed. "He was our best freaking success."

"And we'll get him here." In a cage, if nothing else worked. "Tell the photographer to chill. We'll pay overtime. Then help the staffers with our other clients."

They filled every treatment room tonight. Their hissing, growls and howls proved mild compared to the raucous outside sounds. Despite being ninety degrees with equally high humidity, this street in the French Quarter boomed with life. Tourists, musicians, locals and businesspeople partied hearty, each unaware of what went on in the salon.

"Okay." Zoe slumped and eyed the dust pile on Becca's desk. "Ah...sorry for losing my cool."

"Not a prob. It's a very human trait."

Zoe showed her teeth. For her, that was a grateful smile. Batting smoke away from her face, she trudged to the door, stopped and stared at the ingredients peeking out from behind the potted plants.

She didn't ask what they were doing there or comment about her boss's lousy magic skills.

Becca buzzed the reception desk where Heather, another BFF, greeted, scheduled and rang out customers.

No answer.

"Heather!" Becca wanted her to work on getting the AWOL client here.

Still no response.

Nothing was going right tonight, which made it like the others in their business.

Swearing, Becca hurried down the hall and searched for Heather. She wasn't in the break room. There, two vampires guzzled bottles of imported blood. Their pasty skin was almost rosy from the workout they'd been through.

The guy on the left resembled a young Brad Pitt. He gave her a thumbs-up. The other one, a dead ringer for Colin Farrell, gave her the finger.

Becca pushed out her lower lip. "Tough night, huh?"

He hung his head. "This shit is so hard."

"But worth it, right? You said you wanted that mortal babe who lives down the street from you."

A longing groan poured from him, followed by a gentle sigh. "Unfortunately."

Vamps were so cute when they craved a woman for companionship rather than her plasma. "Who said love would be easy?"

"It could be." Hope shone in his pale gray eyes. "All I have to do is turn her then she'd be mine. For, like, always."

The other vamp nodded in encouragement.

Becca got tough. "Doing that wouldn't be playing fair. That's why you're here."

Although these sorry souls could force mortals to their side for whatever they wanted, including adoration, love like that wasn't earned. It never satisfied for long. Doing things the human way by wooing the girl and winning her over with nothing except their innate charm was more intoxicating than every power the mortal and paranormal world offered.

Becca had witnessed it first-hand with her parents. Years ago, her mom could have cast a spell to snare Wade Salt, the only man she'd ever loved, but she'd let nature take its course. Next month, they'd celebrate their thirtieth anniversary.

A sweet and lasting romance Becca would have liked for herself with a one-in-a-million guy. Wasn't in the cards. When it came to males, she always struck out whether they were paras or human. "I would hope you're not thinking of turning a woman against her will."

The vamps shot guilty looks at each other.

They needed additional workouts. Becca made a mental note to have Heather book them every night next week. She pointed at their bottles. "Don't waste a drop of that stuff. It's expensive."

The one on the left read the label. "Little wonder. Comes from European aristocracy."

If that were true, then Becca was Chaz Bono and Paris Hilton's love child. "Only the best for you guys."

She rushed down the hall. Emblazoned on the walls was the company name, From Crud to Stud. Beneath those words the advertising motto read 'Suppressing the Beast'.

A creature snarled from behind a door on the left.

Heather moaned and made pained noises. "Oh, no. Really no. Please no. Try to relax."

Snapping noises answered her. Skittering sounds followed.

If Becca had to guess, Heather had put distance between herself and the guy's teeth.

Zoe's distinctive growl sounded from inside the room. "Stay over there." Something slammed into the wall. Possibly her fist. "I'll handle him."

A wise plan since Heather was a good fairy whose only power lay in healing. She knew to wait until Zoe had muzzled the guy before fixing whatever he'd hurt.

Wanting Heather out here, Becca raised her fist to knock.

The front door swung open.

Heat and humidity poured inside, along with racket from the street party. Drunken voices mingled with throaty laughter, pounding drums and trumpets. The instruments reached and held their highest notes.

A guy slipped inside. At least six-three, he had an athlete's build—lean and muscular, his shoulders broad, hips narrow, thighs powerful.

Becca's pulse thumped in her ears, drowning out the other sounds. She stepped closer.

Classically handsome, he wore his hair preppy-style, longer on the top, shorter on the sides. Those locks were a warm chestnut brown streaked by the sun and tousled, begging for a woman to smooth them back.

Becca lowered her hand. She hadn't intended to lift it.

His golden complexion spoke of days spent outdoors, perhaps from skinny-dipping in a pool, water streaming over his firm pecs and abs, the dark curls between his legs trapping the moisture, his rock-hard cock jutting out, inflexible as iron, sleek as a spear.

She suppressed a delighted shiver.

He wore leather loafers, beige khakis and a white dress shirt opened at the collar, the sleeves folded back to mid-forearm.

Masculine yet civilized.

The staff had done an outstanding job on this guy's makeover. No wonder Zoe had suggested him for the advertising pieces. A fat raise for everyone was in order. Maybe even part ownership in this place. They'd made this dude over to the nth degree from…

Becca wasn't certain what kind of demon he was or his level in Hell. She'd never met him before. Maybe he'd taken so long to get there because he couldn't pull himself away from the god he now saw in his mirror.

He regarded the reception area as one would when seeing it for a first time or through different eyes…a reformed demon's eyes. Potted plants and feathery ferns abounded. The faux brick floor, coral walls and gas wall fixtures radiated warmth and an earthy, sensual feel in keeping with the area's culture.

It was also romantic.

That was why most paras signed up for the ordeals they'd face here. They were having problems with babes and wanted a solution, even if it was painful.

Hissing noises flowed from a room on the right. On the left, muffled groans sounded faintly sexual.

Could be that was why this guy was late. He'd already seduced a new lover and had been reluctant to leave her.

The thick ridge behind his fly held enormous promise. Some women had all the luck. Becca, on the other hand, had a business to run.

Reining in her desire, she joined him in the reception area. "Do you have any idea how late it is?"

His attention zipped over her. He lifted his eyebrows.

Becca wasn't certain if he was surprised or amused at how unique she looked, from her flame-red hair, cut in a chin-length bob with bangs, to her dramatic makeup. Heavy black liner surrounded her blue eyes. Her maroon lipstick was a shade lighter than black and quite a contrast to her pale skin.

His attention didn't remain on her complexion for long. He was riveted to her black silk top tied beneath her breasts, then her silver navel jewelry, then her black harem pants, anklets, toe rings and high-heel sandals.

Even at five-seven, and with the extra three inches the shoes gave her, Becca felt dainty next to him. Quite a feat, considering she'd always been too tall and curvy. In school, they'd called her the f-word.

Well, fuck 'em, right? So she'd never be skinny or a beauty. Not like her mom. Unfortunately, Becca took after her dad. A great guy, but no hunk in the looks department.

"We can't wait forever." She gestured for the dude to follow her. "Let's go."

She hurried down the hall. Her heels clicked.

His shoes didn't make any noise.

She stopped and looked over. He hadn't taken a step in her direction. He was far too busy studying her ass. Intently and appreciatively if his crooked smile was any indication.

Her heart fluttered.

She hoped his response wasn't something the staff had taught him. Gaining his approval on her own, because he liked what he saw, would be far nicer. "You coming?"

He blushed beneath his tan. What appeared to be carnal hunger sparked in his eyes. "Where?"

His voice was even deeper than those of the howlers that came here for treatment. Way huskier than Zoe's when she got riled. Becca drifted back to him, drawn by his potent masculinity, until she forced herself to stop and pointed over her shoulder.

He approached with grace, though not too much, more like a well-behaved panther. Loose limbed and composed, not cocky or predatory. The employees here were freaking miracle workers.

He stopped close enough for him and Becca to touch or kiss. "Sure."

His eyes were honey colored with green flecks. Given his laugh lines, he looked to be in his early thirties, if she used mortal time. That made him a few years older than her.

Not that their ages mattered. Once his photo shoot ended, he'd take off and would be back in bed with his newest babe, the first of many.

Disappointment rolled through her. "There." She pointed to the side and tried not to drool over him.

He checked her out too and offered another crooked grin. "There what?"

She had no answer. His adorable smile tangled her thoughts. Becca lowered her head and tried to pull in a full breath but couldn't. "Door on the right. Go in that room. Take off your clothes. I'll get the photographer so we can get things started."

She pivoted.

He cuffed her wrist to keep her from leaving.

The spit in her mouth dried up.

He leaned in. "What?"

That voice. His touch. Her knees sagged. With great effort, Becca faced him.

He gave her a questioning look.

She wanted to ruffle his long dark lashes, kiss his silky eyebrows and suck his lower lip into her mouth while she crawled all over him. "Briefs or boxers?"

He pulled back slightly, but didn't release her wrist. "What?"

She cleared her throat. "What are you wearing?" Her voice jiggled and rasped. "Briefs or boxers?"

He looked down at his clothing. "Boxers."

"The stretchy kind or the baggy ones?"

He released her wrist, offense on his handsome face. "They're not that baggy."

She'd hurt his feelings. A nice human touch the staff must have taught him. Like having him stare at a female's ass, rather than grabbing it as demons were prone to do. A man who controlled his inner beast made a woman feel respected yet also sexy and desired. "I'm sure they're not. Still, we prefer the snug ones."

The kind that would hug his fleshy balls and caress his rigid cock. On wobbly legs, Becca crossed to the hall closet and pulled out a navy pair.

"Here." She flung them at him.

They landed on his deliciously broad shoulder.

Becca backed up. "Strip down, then put those on. We can't screw around any longer."

"Sure about that?"

She turned away before he could see her smile. "Completely. Now get—"

A snarl stopped her.

He'd opened the wrong door. Two female staffers held down an alpha shifter they were treating with moonlight therapy. Slobber dripped from his mouth. He growled, battling his compulsion to morph into a werewolf.

The staffer on the right panted. "That's it, baby. Fight it. You can do this."

The guy sprouted unsightly hair even on his balding head.

"No, no, no." The staffer on the left clenched her jaw. "Don't do that. You want to take moonlight strolls with your girl, right? Come on, work with me here."

Becca shut the door and gave Mr. Stud a smile. "Wrong room." She rested her hand on his back. Stone wasn't as solid as his muscles. She blew out a breath. "Next one." She guided him to it and opened the door. "In there."

"If you say so."

The staff had really housebroken him.

Becca inched closer. His scent was as heady as his rich baritone, a cedar, musk and rum fragrance. "I do. Go."

She planted her hand on his chest and pushed.

He was too big and solid to budge. Dutifully, he backed into the room. His thigh hit a table. The desk lamp tottered.

Becca fought a smile. "Careful. Be back in a sec."

She closed the door before she surrendered to her lust and slipped inside to help him undress.

Breathing hard, she pinched her nose and tried to get a grip. What in the hell was the matter with her? Although she'd fallen for weres, vamps, demons and countless other jerks in the past, she'd sworn off all males for the time being, not wanting to get her heart and self-esteem pulverized again.

The staff might have changed this guy on the outside, but inside he was still a predator. The ultimate bad boy—charming, seductive and totally into himself. Selfish as fucking hell. Nothing like her dad.

Too bad mortals didn't appeal to her.

Muttering a curse, Becca stomped down the hall and stopped.

A new guy had arrived. His black tee could have been skin, the fabric hugged his outstanding torso that well. He wore biker boots and faded jeans slung low. His crotch was nicely filled out, that bulge one of the Seven Wonders of the World. He sported a Celtic tat on his muscular forearm, the design geometric and powerful. His midnight hair hung over his forehead. He gave her an Elvis-type smile, upper lip curled seductively. "Hey there."

He made it sound like "Let's screw".

"Ah…hi." Confused as to who he was, Becca stepped closer.

Faint flames danced in his dark eyes.

She sucked in a breath. There hadn't been any fire in the other guy's pupils…at least the literal kind.

"Sorry, I'm late." This dude edged so close his groin almost kissed hers. "I was delayed with other stuff." He grinned indecently. "You know."

Unfortunately, Becca did. She turned to the hall.

He slung his arm over her shoulder. His fingers dangled close to her right nipple. His lips brushed her ear. "So, what now?"

"Don't move." Becca shoved his arm off her and rushed to the guy she'd thought the staff had made over. They hadn't. The service's 'best freaking success' was in the reception area behaving like a bull during a rut. More civilized than he'd been before, but not as much as the man she'd told to strip.

Becca had no idea who in the fuck he could be.

Not bothering to knock, she pushed in the door.

He was naked as the day he'd been born, the boxer briefs mid-thigh, leaving his male package swinging in the breeze—mouth-watering balls, plump as plums, and a long cock protruding from his thatch of brown curls.

Becca squeezed the doorknob so hard her palm hurt.

He didn't move, except for one part. His rod thickened and grew even longer, the crown firm, engorged from desire. The damn thing pointed at her.

Like a zombie detecting fresh meat, she stepped closer, attracted to his masculine goods, wanting them.

"Becca?" *Heather.*

Of all the times for her to show up.

Heather leaned into the room until she saw Mr. Stud. "Oh...oh."

Wow was the word Becca would have used. He'd gotten harder. The prominent veins on his shaft bulged.

Becca elbowed Heather away. On a breathy gasp, she stepped back.

"Sorry." Becca gave him a weak smile. "I didn't know...that is...I thought..."

"I was someone else?"

She nodded then frowned. "Who are you?"

He yanked the boxers up. The elastic waistband caught on his balls.

That had to have hurt.

He sucked air through his clenched teeth and hurried the underwear past his groin. Before he got it over his tight ass, he lost his footing. Trying to regain it, he jerked around.

There was a heart, the perfect Cupid's kind, on his right butt cheek.

Chapter Two

Staggering this way and that, Eric Diletto yanked the underwear up and prayed the redhead would leave before he made a complete ass of himself.

The door swung shut.

He twisted, somehow righted himself and pulled a muscle in his back.

White-hot pain slashed through him.

He bent at the waist and gulped air.

Her heels tapped as they would if she were stepping away from the room.

Wasting no time, he jerked on his khakis and was still hopping on one foot when he noticed his baggy green boxers crumpled on the floor.

He'd forgotten to take off the underwear she'd thrown at him, proving he wasn't only stupid for having put it on but a full-fledged imbecile for following her orders. His head fell forward. He let out a pissed groan.

"You okay?" She rapped lightly on the door.

"Fine!" He lowered his voice. "Just getting dressed."

Her heels tapped faster. "Oh...well, sure. That's okay."

As if it wouldn't have been if he'd decided otherwise? He liked the hesitation and regret lacing her words. Maybe she was torn as to whether to stay out there or come back in here and enjoy the show.

Or laugh.

His pain and embarrassment returned. Dismissing both, Eric planted his hands on his hips and thought back to how she'd looked when his junk had hung free. Stunned, sure, but also aroused. The way a woman would behave if she wanted to fall to her knees and lick him.

With her, that would be uber nice. His wide grin hurt his cheeks.

Something rammed into the wall behind him.

"Don't. Do. That." The woman's voice couldn't have been more gravelly unless she'd gargled with Drāno.

A hiss from Hell answered her. Pounding shook the photos hanging in here. Each depicted the French Quarter. Weird symbols graced the edges. In Greek? Martian? Who knew?

Despite the redhead's allure and strange hold on him, Eric figured it was definitely time to break out of this looney bin.

He shoved his feet into his loafers and pulled on his shirt but didn't bother to button the damn thing. With his boxers dangling from his front pocket, he inched to the door and put his ear against it.

Muted howls, shrieks and groans greeted him.

He hoped he wouldn't have to fight his way out. He knew some martial arts but wasn't a whiz at it like Neo who'd spun like a human tornado in *The Matrix*. Hell, Eric wasn't even a beast, which was why he'd come here in the first place. A move that had turned out to be fucking dumb and possibly dangerous to his safety.

Cursing himself, he edged the door open.

The redhead was gone.

Her fragrance lingered. Something deep, seductive and witchy, for lack of a better word. The scent brought to mind sultry nights, rustling black silk and delightful female musk.

He trembled with need and wrinkled his nose at another smell. The stink that burnt matches made.

No way did he want to know where that came from. He slipped into the hall and closed the door carefully to avoid making any noise. Not that anyone would notice given the commotion in the other rooms. Bangs, snaps, growls and hisses mingled with female voices begging or cooing. Some of those women sounded older than Death. Others spoke lightly and musically.

The normal voices weren't as nice as the redhead's throaty purr. Her impact on Eric's cock lingered. The damn thing was on the prowl, getting too thick, trying to snake out of his snug boxers and go straight to…where? Her?

Like that would happen after he escaped.

Ignoring his idiotic desire, he strode down the hall to the front door and stopped short.

The young woman who stood between him and freedom looked to be about fourteen and dressed in a schoolgirl's uniform—plaid skirt, white blouse, saddle shoes. She crossed her arms over her flat chest and shook her head at him. Flames flared in her eyes.

His blood turned to ice.

A sulfur stench hit.

He made a face at the unpleasant odor.

She scrunched her nose, too, either smelling what he had or could be she was mocking him. The piercings on her face glinted.

He forced a smile and risked another step toward her. "Excuse me. You're in my way."

"You think?" She glowered. "You're not leaving."

Eric hoped he could take her. She was a little thing, but the smoke rising from her hair and shoulders might present a problem. She could mutate into something worse than whatever hit the walls in this place. The pictures up here bounced.

He tried to reason. "I have another appointment. I'm expected."

She bared her teeth at his lie.

"Seriously." He squared his shoulders to look bigger than he was and far crazier than her. "If I don't show up—"

"You can leave." The redhead spoke from the side. "We have no intention of keeping you here."

He turned at her husky, sexier-than-sin promise.

She leaned against the wall. Her attention darted from his boxers, crammed into his pocket, to what she could see of his naked chest. She lingered there and ran her maroon-polished nail over her belly button.

Eric's bones nearly liquefied. He wanted to lick her sweet navel, tongue the silver butterfly dangling from it and move lower to the pleasure beneath her loose-fitting pants. His cock twitched and grew another inch or two. Blood thickened it.

Her cheeks pinked up. "However, before you do leave, you and I have to talk."

The schoolgirl chuckled. A sound somewhere between a hissing snake and a growling lion that only the damned should hear.

"In my office." The redhead gestured. "Please."

Her murmur drew Eric closer, though, he did halt several feet away. He was turned on, not nuts. "Why?"

"I'll explain in my office. I promise you'll be safe. No harm will come to you."

He didn't budge.

She smiled sweetly. "You have my word. I'm Becca Salt. This is my place."

As if he hadn't already guessed as much when she'd ordered him to strip then thrown the stretchy boxers at him.

She offered her hand. Her fingers were long, her skin plump with youth, looking softer than a baby's butt.

Eric vacillated between arousal and fear but took the plunge and slipped his palm over hers. Something jolted through him, similar to a mild electric shock. He hoped it was from his attraction to her and not because she was preparing to strike him dead.

She squeezed his hand tenderly. Lovingly.

His legs bowed. Her touch generated more heat than a slug of good booze. Her velvety soft skin encouraged him to caress her fingers. "Ms. Salt."

"Becca, please. And you are?"

Uncertain as shit about this. That didn't mean he wasn't enjoying it. "Eric. Um, Diletto."

He tensed, prepared for her to react to his family name.

She didn't. Instead, she regarded him with openness and honesty.

Despite her weird makeup, she had amazing eyes, so blue the color didn't seem real. Her pillowy lips were definitely kissable even with her strange lipstick, while her features were striking. Better than pretty. Interesting.

The walls shook.

She gave him an edgy smile. "Let's go to my office. It's much quieter there."

He trailed after her and looked over to see if the schoolgirl had followed.

She stood at the front door, teeth gritted and shoulders tensed, keeping him from escape.

"Here we go." Becca gestured him inside.

Her office contained more greenery than the reception area and faced the noisy street. Several guys duked it out down there, their shouts and curses flying fast. Their ladies squealed or screeched at how they were doing. A piercing shriek from a whistle cut them off. Definitely not quieter in here, but at least the sounds were ordinary.

Eric brushed past several ferns and other plants he couldn't begin to identify, their scents rich and sensual. Those pleasant odors mingled with another fresh and inviting fragrance, similar to newly mown grass.

Numerous bottles and bowls filled with unknown herbs, spices or something else crowded around the potted plants. Maybe to ward off bugs or to perfume this room further.

"Please have a seat." Becca swung her hand to the needlepoint sofa that faced her antique desk.

As a financial analyst, Eric had been in enough mansions to know real when he saw it. The furniture designs, ornate inlays and gold ornamentation put them at approximately the seventeenth century, possibly gifts from Louis XIV himself. Her Tiffany floor lamp was genuine, too, not a knockoff hawked on the Home Shopping Network.

She'd decorated this room with care, but impersonally, no family photos showing kids or a husband. No boyfriends, either, or pets. However her space owned a homey, comfortable feel.

Eric hoped that wasn't to snare in the unsuspecting. The dust pile on her desk gave him pause. He hoped it was crumbs from countless powdered sugar donuts and not drugs.

He sank to the sofa. Its stiff cushion was as uncomfortable as he felt.

Becca closed the door and rounded her desk. She regarded the street scene, tourists and locals enjoying themselves or getting into trouble, going about their lives.

Her intercom buzzed. She depressed a button. "No interruptions, please."

A whimper sounded from the other end. "Sure. Sorry. Really, I am. I shouldn't have bothered you and I won't again, until you say I should. I promise I'll —"

"It's okay, Heather. No interruptions, all right?"

"Sure. Sorry. I —"

Becca cut the transmission off and faced him. "I want to apologize for what happened tonight. I honestly believed you were a client. We'd arranged a photo shoot for him. He was late. When you showed up, I thought..."

She stared at his chest.

He still hadn't buttoned his shirt. "Do you want me to finish dressing?"

"Oh, no." She smiled dreamily. "Hell, no." She met his gaze and blinked. Her cheeks turned the same shade as a ripe peach. "I mean, button your shirt or don't button it. Either way, it doesn't bother me."

Eric smiled at her lie.

Her blush deepened. She cleared her throat. "We have to talk."

The air conditioning kicked on. The chilled breeze spread the dust. She brushed it into a wastebasket, slapped her hands together then sank to her elaborate chair and rested her hands on the desk, fingers laced. The pose every boss affects right before firing the poor soul facing him.

Eric hadn't a clue what she wanted to talk about. He scooted to the cushion edge. "Go on."

Becca sucked her bottom lip.

His skin tingled. He wanted to suck her lip for her. "Hey." He empathized with how uncertain she looked. He'd been that way around women his entire existence. "I'm easy to talk to. Really."

She moaned. A soft, female sound that was totally adorable.

He fought a smile...at this point she might think he was making fun of her. He'd chew off his nuts first. "Yes?"

She drooped. "I hate to say this, but we need to remove your memories of your time here. I promise it won't hurt at all."

Eric stood.

Or rather, he shot to his feet. The sofa bumped over the brick floor and smacked into the wall.

Becca wanted to comfort him but figured he wouldn't listen.

Escape was etched on his face.

The door swung open. Zoe blocked him, her hair and shoulders belching smoke like Mount St. Helens before it blew.

He backed away from her and frowned at Becca. "Is she about to catch fire?"

"Everything's perfectly all right." Becca gave him a reassuring smile.

The face he made said she was insane. "Are you serious? You said you want to remove my memories, or have you forgotten that?"

"Please sit." She gestured him down.

He stayed well away from the sofa and Zoe, buttoned his shirt and shoved the tails into his khakis.

If there was such a thing as sin, what he'd just done met the criteria. He had an outstanding chest he should never cover. His other stuff was great, too. The treasure behind his fly looked harder than steel. Undoubtedly hot and scented with his musk.

Her head swam.

"I have to leave." He shifted his weight. "Now."

"In a minute, after we talk." Becca spoke to Zoe. "Please leave us alone."

"If you need me, holler." She glared at Eric, swaggered out and slammed the door.

He pointed at Becca. "You're not taking anything from me. Got it?"

She understood his aversion and tried to soothe. "We won't hurt you."

"Yeah, right. Are you on something?"

"What?"

"That stuff you scraped from your desk. Looked like drugs to me."

She didn't much like his attitude or accusation. "No one here does that stuff." Narcotics were a mortal thing. Paras had innate abilities to deal with their shit, except when it came to love. Then they could revert to dark powers to get what they wanted and ease their pain. For her, chocolate worked, except for making her thighs and butt even bigger. "The dust was simply what remained of a book that disintegrated."

"Sure. Why would it do that?"

Even a gun to her face wouldn't make her confess. "Look, we're not going to hurt you in any way, shape or form."

"Except to slice out part of my brain to get rid of my memories."

She resisted the urge to roll her eyes. "Only those of you being here. There's no surgery involved. We're not zoned for that. Constance will simply —"

"Constance?"

Another BFF and voodoo priestess who worked there. "Don't worry. She's a staff member, fully licensed in her field."

"Which is?"

The shit voodoo priestesses did. "Helping others. She'll lay her hands on your head and —"

"No."

Becca squeezed her fingers so hard her knuckles hurt. "Please try to understand. You've seen things here that you really shouldn't have."

"Says who? I came here for a makeover, all right?"

She leaned against her desk. "Seriously? You're not mortal?"

"If I were, would I be in this nuthouse?"

A client's piercing howl tore through the premises and quieted.

She fingered her top. "What are you?" He wasn't a demon or a vamp. However, a were or other shifter wasn't implausible. "Exactly what?"

"I'm Eric. Di-let-to."

He'd pronounced his last name ultra slow, as though that should mean something to her.

It wasn't ringing a bell. "Okay."

"No, it's not. I haven't always gone by Eric. I changed my first name when I was twelve. Got tired of having to fight the other kids, you know?"

Becca did. She'd had her own scuffles when anyone had dared call her fat. Compassion and tenderness for him mingled with her building lust. "Tell me your real first name. Please."

He sagged to the sofa. "You'll laugh."

"Never." She hurried around her desk.

He leaned away from her.

Becca stopped. No way did she want him to feel more unglued than he already was or to make a fool of herself by being too forward. "I don't make fun. I don't bully. I had enough of that when I was a child to know how much it hurts."

He nodded sympathetically. "The other kids made fun of your hair, huh?"

"No." She curled her upper lip. "There's something wrong with my hair?"

He held up his hands in appeasement. "Not at all. I really like the color and the way you wear it." He gestured to his own head to demonstrate her bob and bangs. "It's great."

Sure, and Santa Claus is a card-carrying Communist. "The other kids made fun of my weight." There, she'd said it. Little need to pretend there wasn't a four-ton elephant in the room.

"Really?" He took her in, loitering on her ample cleavage and curvy hips. "I don't see how. You're perfect. Most women today are too skinny."

Honesty shone on his face.

Becca liked that and what he'd said. "What's your real first name?"

He lay on the sofa, arm draped over his eyes. He looked like a patient unwilling to confess his innermost thoughts to a shrink.

"Come on." She used her gentlest tone. "We can't help you if you don't tell us what the problem is. It can't be that bad."

"Wanna bet? My real first name is Eros."

With lightning speed, the pieces fell together for Becca. His last name was Diletto. Italian for pleasure. She recalled the tat on his ass. He was an honest-to-fuck Greek god, or technically a Roman one. "You come from the line of Psyche and Eros."

"Yeah, I know." He growled. "Unfortunately, Eros has a nickname."

"Cupid?"

"Bingo. But that's not the one the kids in middle school used. There, I was known as 'we're-gonna-pound-your-pussy-ass-into-the-ground'. I tried to tell my parents that sending me to a regular school was nuts, but did they listen? No. They wanted me to have a well-rounded education and childhood. Unfortunately, it included countless bruises, scrapes and black eyes from mortals who thought I was beyond weird. There you have it. That's what I wanted to run from back then and sure as hell don't want to repeat in the present or future."

Becca gave him a moment to calm down.

His huffs quieted somewhat.

"I'm confused." She edged closer. "Given how you feel, why'd you get a heart tattooed on your butt?"

"It's not a tat. It's a birthmark. I went to several laser specialists. They worked on it dozens of times. Stupid thing keeps coming back." He tightened his shoulders. "You shouldn't have seen it."

She wasn't sorry. "Forgive me?"

He shrugged.

"I'm still confused. Clearly, since you changed your name, that's not a problem any longer. I'm guessing you don't show your birthmark to mortal women until you get to know them at least moderately well."

He shot her a look.

Even irritated, he was awesome. "What I'm trying to get at is that From Crud to Stud helps clients to suppress their beast. You don't have one. You're a perfect gentleman. Outwardly normal to mortals." Except for his birthmark, of course, which Becca wasn't crazy enough to mention again. That would be cruel. "What in the world could you want to change?"

"Ever hear the term 'nice guys finish last'?"

"Are you saying that you're losing out on the babes because you're too nice?" That was impossible. He was gorgeous, kind, funny, hung…

"Women say they want a nice guy, but they don't really."

Now, she'd heard it all. If one more guy tried to mansplain a woman's feelings to her… She crossed her arms beneath her breasts. "When was the last time you were on my side of the fence, so to speak?"

"Never. I don't have to be. I've dated hundreds of females to know how they operate."

He had to be bragging. Maybe. "Hundreds?"

"If I'd told you the truth, that it was thousands, you wouldn't have believed me."

Jealousy twisted Becca's gut when it shouldn't have. He wasn't anything to her. She'd never be anything to him. Hot guys like Eric breezed by her as they would the invisible woman. "Thousands? And they all dumped you?"

"Not right away." Misery crossed his face.

Becca felt like a shit for causing him any pain. "Sorry, I didn't mean to sound so…"

"Bitchy?"

"Sure, we'll go with that." She pushed her bangs off her forehead.

"I really do like your hair color." Admiration sparkled in his eyes.

Warmth poured through her so quickly she perspired. The last time she'd been this flustered around a guy was in tenth grade when the football captain had accidentally shoved her into a locker and blurted, "Sorry. Didn't see you."

It wasn't his apology that had enthralled, but the way he'd said it. As though he'd considered her a human being. Not an inanimate object.

Eric focused on her to the exclusion of everything else. Not even the weird sounds pouring from the other rooms distracted him.

Becca wasn't certain if his attention was real because of the person she was or was due to his innate genetic charm. Somehow, she didn't want to know and risk disappointment. She'd had enough of that to fill several lifetimes. "Are you saying you want us to release your beast? That is, if you have any."

"I do." He pushed to a sitting position. "Hell, I must. No one's perfect."

He was pretty damn close. "You want us to make you rude, obnoxious, selfish, vulgar, condescending and basically unbearable like our other clients are when they first come here?"

"I don't want to offend. But, hey, a little of that stuff wouldn't hurt."

She rubbed her forehead. "I think you have the wrong idea about women. We really do want an honorable man. Someone who's kind."

"Have you ever married one?"

No one had come close to asking. "No."

He glanced at her ringless fingers. "Ever been engaged to a guy like that?"

"Look—"

"I'll take that as a no. That leaves dating. Are you currently tight with a nice guy?"

Her face heated. "My personal life isn't up for discussion."

"Then you've proved my point, you're with a mean mother —"

"No."

"Hmm. I'm not involved with anyone, either. But I guess you already know that since I'm here." He searched her face. "So tell me, when you were dating a nice guy, how long did the magic last? I'm talking figuratively here."

In that case, her answer would have to be far too briefly. She'd always fallen for the bad boys, delighted when they threw some attention her way. For some weird reason, she was determined to turn their scant attraction into everlasting love. Never happened. They used her. She got hurt, swore never to be a victim again then offered herself up as a new sacrifice to another SOB. Except for the last six months. Becca had kept her pledge not to be screwed, hadn't had sex in half a year and was ready to jump out of her skin, especially around Eric. Wasn't going to happen with him. "Let me make this clear, we are not talking about me."

"Fair enough. Let's ask your staff how they feel about nice guys."

"Zoe's sworn off men and sex."

"Zoe?"

"The young woman who was just in here, smoking up a storm."

"Ah. Given her attitude, it's lucky for guys she's not into them any longer."

Becca twisted her mouth.

"Careful." He wagged his finger. "Your face might freeze that way."

She was not going to smile.

Eric inclined his head to the hall. "Have you been listening to that?"

"The groans and howls?" To Becca they were background noise.

"No. The conversation."

She opened the door.

Four staff members huddled by a treatment room and giggled worse than tweens. Constance, who was young, black and beautiful, wore her signature turban and flowing gown. Tonight's ensemble was in peacock blue and iridescent green. Next to colorful Constance, Heather looked even more delicate than the typical fairy. At least, those envisioned by artists and Hollywood. Although Heather was five-six or so and didn't have wings, she was so blonde, pale and slender she seemed in danger of fading away. The other two staff members, Hope and Faith, were tiger shifters and twins Becca could never tell apart.

"We really shouldn't change him." Constance grinned. "He's fine just as he is."

Hope, or maybe Faith, pressed her hands to her chest and sighed. "I love how he knows what he wants and tells me. Gets right to the freaking point, amirite?"

"Fuck yeah." Faith, or maybe Hope, wiggled her slender eyebrows. "When he growls an order, I can't move fast enough. Imagine what he'd be like in bed."

"Along with his outstanding tail." The first one moaned. "Imagine the places it'd take you."

Constance nodded knowingly. "He's one helluva demon. Talk about a deep voice. I bet women can hear him in the next parish. Wow."

Heather blushed. "He is cute."

"Cute, my ass." Constance sniggered. "Try sexy as sin. Commanding as hell. Did you see his muscles? His thighs? That cock?"

"Constance, please." Heather shook her head. "No need to talk like that."

"Why not? His thing is downright lethal. At least a foot long if not more."

"See? I was right."

Becca started at Eric's voice.

He was behind her, whispering in her ear. "They prefer beasts, not nice guys."

His breath was fresh and minty, not to mention hot and thrilling. A few inches closer and his shaft would snuggle against her ass.

Becca fought a delighted moan and closed the door. "That's just talk. Like guys do in locker rooms."

He stepped away. "That may be, but it's also my reality. Every time I get serious about a woman, she dumps me for some mean prick, figuratively and literally. I'm tired of it. I want you to release my inner beast."

Becca gestured helplessly. "We don't have the tools in place to do that."

"Sure you do. Whatever you're using on your clients now, simply reverse the process for me."

She sagged against the door. "None of my staff has ever done anything like that before."

"Who cares? I don't want them. I want you. In fact, I'm demanding you."

Becca didn't know how to respond. Other than her parents, she couldn't recall anyone wanting her above everyone else. Unsettled, she fingered her blouse above her cleavage.

Eric watched. The impressive ridge between his legs got a little plumper, surely harder. A knee-jerk reaction? Genuine interest?

She still wasn't certain. "Me?"

"Yup. You."

"Why?"

He regarded her. Gone was the nice guy, the boyish grin and gentle teasing. In its place was a man who knew what he wanted, no different from the demon Zoe had selected for the photoshoot. "Why else? You own this place. Presumably, you're the best."

"Not presumably." At least as far as business acumen went. Everything else? No freaking way.

"Good. We agree on something."

"I haven't agreed to anything."

"You will. I'll pay you ten times what the others do." He approached her, loose-limbed and confident like before, but also a tad predatory.

Becca waffled between standing her ground and sidling away. She opted for the latter.

He followed. "You're going to bring out my inner beast and turn me into one fucking bad boy for all those women out there. Babes I intend to meet and keep for a change."

Chapter Three

Becca entered her parents' house laden with Chinese takeout and too many questions on witchcraft. She loved her mom and dad, but they weren't who she wanted to see tonight. Too bad she wasn't a babe that Eric would get down and dirty with for an extended period like he wanted, or rather, demanded. "Hey, guys. I'm here."

Her attempt to sound upbeat came out flat.

Dishes rattled in the kitchen. Her mother getting stuff ready for meals as she always had, exactly as a mortal wife would.

"Mom?"

"Coming." Rowena hurried into the entry hall. Streetlights bled through the Victorian stained-glass windows, splashing color on the rose walls and her mom's black outfit—a stretchy ballet top and capris that defined sexy and showed off her perfect hourglass figure.

She was impressive by mortal standards, yet her great looks were expected for a five-hundred-year-old witch.

Although she hadn't aged a day in centuries, she did have several silver streaks in her short black hair, laugh lines gracing her gray eyes and faintly drooping jowls. The results of spells she'd cast on herself for Becca's dad. In this youth-obsessed world, Rowena insisted on aging beside him even though he'd never asked her to do so.

If the devotion they shared wasn't love, Becca hadn't a clue what might be.

"What took you so long? You're late." Rowena hugged her.

Becca returned the greeting and savored her mom's scent. Johnson's baby powder. Her dad had liked the fragrance so much during Becca's infancy, Rowena had taken to sprinkling the stuff on herself.

"What's wrong?" She cupped Becca's face. Her elaborate silver rings, two on each finger, were slightly cooler than her palms. "What happened?"

"Nothing." She shook the huge take-out bag. "They were really busy at Happy Wok." Her parent's favorite restaurant. "I had to wait forever for the order."

"I'm sure you did. But do you want to tell me the real reason you look so sad?"

Not if it meant mentioning Eric. Too bad he'd given her little choice. Becca fought melancholy and slapped on a smile. "I'm not sad. And you don't have to worry about anything else, either. I didn't cast any spells at the restaurant, hoping to hurry the order along. I've learned my lesson about invoking powers in public. Privately, I have been practicing."

"That's wonderful! How'd it go?"

Becca told her. "Those stupid books need to be updated for the modern world. I followed every freaking instruction to the letter and the spells still messed up. As far as the advertisement goes, I'm convinced that would have happened no matter what I did."

"It would have. However, the other missteps are because of your attitude. Magic knows when you're not serious or if you're bored by it."

Becca didn't believe that for a minute. "Maybe we should just face facts. No way will I ever be good at conjuring like you are. My mortal side gets in the way."

"Baloney. You could achieve whatever you wanted if you respected your craft and studied harder."

"And miss *Dancing with the Stars*?"

"You joke now, but someday you might need it."

Someday was this minute. Becca slumped.

Rowena regarded her. "There is something wrong. Do you want to talk about it?"

Wanting and needing to were different matters. Not that she planned to get into the subject, or rather, Eric, now. "Everything's cool. Honestly."

"Then we'll talk about other stuff. Catch up. Say hi to your dad and meet me in the kitchen." She kissed Becca's nose and gave her a look that said she could read her soul. "Okay?"

It wasn't. She had to stop giving away her feelings to her mom and Eric. He'd regarded her the same way Rowena was doing now. Becca handed the bag over. "I'll be right there."

Her dad was in the family room, aka his man cave, his stockinged feet propped on the footrest of his La-Z-Boy recliner. The Times-Picayune lay across his blue-jeaned legs. His scowl was on a Fox News show he loved to bitch at. He muttered at the talking heads on the big-screen TV.

Becca smiled. Her dad still resembled the trucker he'd once been, burly yet cuddly. Since meeting her mom, he'd established and built his own trucking company and made it succeed with backbreaking work, not magic. Although they could have lived in a mega-mansion, given her mom's powers, he wouldn't consider it. Their Victorian home was beautiful, right down to its gingerbread embellishments and wraparound porch, but still modest by immortal standards.

The only time Becca recalled him asking Rowena to use her witchy talent was during the 2010 Super Bowl, played by the New Orleans Saints. She'd refused. The Saints had won anyway.

Becca kissed the top of his head. His bristly salt-and-pepper crewcut tickled her nose. She rubbed it. "Isn't watching that crap bad for your blood pressure?"

"Someone's gotta keep an eye on those fools." He lifted his face to Becca. His Old Spice aftershave wafted in her direction. "Crap?"

She stroked his frown marks. "Dad, I'm twenty-seven, all right? I know all the bad words. I even use them sometimes."

"I hope not in front of guys. Trust me, they like a lady."

Not the beasts she knew. Every time her staff let loose with gutter talk, the clients liked it so much they got humongous hard-ons.

Becca sensed Eric wasn't any different deep, deep down. He'd become assertive when he insisted she help him. Once she'd caved and agreed, he returned to being Mr. Nice Guy. Finishing last with thousands of babes he'd already dated, while millions more waited for the bad boy he wanted to become.

Rowena breezed into the room holding a tray laden with spring rolls, Crab Rangoon, deep-fried wontons and Hui Guo Rou. A Bud Light rounded out the fare. "Here you go."

She placed the feast on his lap, tucked a linen napkin beneath his chin and slipped her arm through Becca's. "We'll be in the kitchen if you need us."

He nodded, his attention torn between dinner and the junk on Fox News.

In the brick-and-brass kitchen, Rowena held up a bottle of red Bordeaux and a Bud Light. "Pick your poison."

Becca wanted neither. Hard liquor, rather than her usual chocolate, called to her, though, not until her escape from here. She gestured to the Bud Light.

Rowena heaped Chinese fare on Becca's plate. "Say when."

"About five spoonfuls ago. Please, enough — thanks."

For the first time in forever, Becca wasn't hungry. Nervous energy ate at her, along with mounting depression. She found it hard to move, but impossible to keep still or quiet. "Do you have any spells to turn a guy into a bad boy?"

Rowena sank to her chair at the wrought-iron table. Behind her, tall windows stretched to the ceiling and showed the balmy night outside. Distant headlights twinkled like lightning bugs. She lowered her serving spoon to the glass top. The metal utensil tinged. "I knew something had happened." She leaned closer. "Who is he?"

Becca pushed back in her chair. "Just a client."

Rowena studied her as she had when Becca was a child, searching for a lie.

She guzzled her beer and belched. "Sorry."

"Is it serious?"

"My belch? Naw. I simply drank this too fast." She held up her bottle.

Rowena shot her a look. "Don't be cute. I'm talking about whatever's going on between you and this client.

Wait." She held up her hand. Her rings glittered in the glow coming from the filigreed ceiling fixture. "Why would you have to turn him into a bad boy if he's one of your customers?"

"It's complicated."

"That's okay." She patted Becca's hand. "I have all night."

"Really complicated."

"I'm available from now until the end of next week if you need it." She crossed her arms on the table. "I'm guessing you're trying to change him from being nice to being a beast. Why would you want to do that?"

"It was his idea, not mine."

"Why?"

Becca hated to say. Even thinking about Eric's plan hurt more than it should, given she barely knew him and wouldn't see him again once he'd reached his goal. She sagged in her chair. The fabric cushion whooshed with her weight. "So, the babes he dates don't keep dumping him for being too considerate or honorable or you name it. Understandably, he's tired of losing out to pricks — that is, other men."

Rowena ignored Becca's colorful language. "Who said he's losing? Those women are clearly too dense to know what's good for them. He sounds perfect to me. What about you? Don't you like him the way he is?"

No sane woman could resist. Becca finished her beer and suppressed a belch. "He's a frigging Greek god."

Rowena smiled. "A real hunk, huh?"

She hadn't a clue. But then she hadn't seen his muscular pecs, thick cock, weighty balls, firm ass and that precious birthmark.

Becca wanted to lick the damn thing and his sac. If ever there was flesh created for a female to worship, a guy's nuts fit the bill, especially Eric's. Short, dark hairs roughened the wrinkly skin and provided a wonderful contrast to his silky crown. What a mouthful it would make.

Her belly fluttered.

She fought her wayward emotions, unwilling to take a fruitless journey with heartache as the destination. Eric had proved that with the last things he'd said. He wanted to change for all the women out there. Them. Not her. Babes he intended to date and keep, until he moved on.

"He's definitely hot." Listlessly, Becca bit into a spring roll. Its taste didn't register. "But he's also an actual Greek god, or rather, a Roman one. A descendant of Cupid and Psyche. He has a heart-shaped birthmark on his — ah, leg — to prove it. His parents named him Eros. He's gone by Eric since he was twelve. Finally got tired of the other boys pounding him into the ground."

"You like him." Delight lit Rowena's face. "About time you went for a nice guy like Dad."

Becca forced down the food in her mouth. "He's a client, Mom. He wants me to change him so he won't only attract the babes — according to him there have been thousands — but he'll also be able to keep them."

"What does he think about you?"

Her laughter filled the room. "I'm not even in the equation."

"Do you want to be?"

She sobered. "No."

Rowena drummed the table. "You're sure?"

Becca figured it was time to confess what was painfully obvious to her and should have been to everyone else, even a loving mother. "He's way out of my league. I'm not gorgeous like you. I'm not built like you."

"Oh, baby." She cradled Becca's face. "You're more beautiful than you can imagine, and there's not one thing wrong with your figure."

"Except that I'm built like Dad or one of his truckers."

"Nonsense. You resemble the beautiful redhead who used to star in *Mad Men*."

Becca chuckled weakly. "I wish."

"Stop talking like that. You're smart, kind, successful and so many other wonderful things I don't have enough days to name all of them. If he doesn't notice you, then he's a fool." She searched Becca's face. "Did he notice you?"

He had smiled at her ass and been riveted by her cleavage. He'd said he liked her hair color. "I don't know. Maybe."

"How? What happened? What did he say?"

Becca waved her hands. "He was probably being nice. It's in his genetic makeup. He comes from the God of love, sweetness, charm and all that other shit."

"Becca."

"Sorry. All that other crap?"

Rowena hung her head.

"Mom, I don't think I ever want to be in love."

"What? Why not?" She held Becca's hand between hers. "Why would you think such a thing?"

She pulled in her shoulders.

"Come on, tell me, baby."

"I can't."

"Why?"

"I don't want to hurt you."

Rowena straightened. Confusion, concern, disbelief and finally acceptance, mingled with sorrow, raced across her lovely features. "You don't like guys?"

She barked a laugh.

Her mother dropped Becca's hand and frowned. Something she seldom did.

"Sorry. Yeah, I still like guys. A lot. Maybe too much."

"Then what's the problem?"

Again, the obvious, at least to her. Although Becca had never brought up the subject, she felt it hung over their household and muted everyone's happiness. No different from the last hours spent with a loved one, trying to be brave and cheerful when you knew you'd never see them again. "What are you going to do when Dad's gone?"

He hadn't a millionth time her mom had.

The color drained from Rowena's face. She focused on her food, pushing it around the crystal plate rather than eating.

"I'm sorry." Becca squeezed her mom's hand. "I don't mean to hurt you. I can't help but worry."

"I know." Rowena cleared her throat and blinked away tears. "When the time comes, which won't be for decades, I'll be fine. I'll have all the wonderful memories we've made. I'll have you."

That didn't cut it. Becca would never be a substitute for her dad. And there was no telling how long she'd be around. She might be immortal like her mom, limited to decades like her dad or somewhere in between. No one freaking knew. "Damn, love sucks."

Rowena laughed and cried. She swiped at her tears and growled, "It's worth it. Every lousy, cruddy, crappy, shitty minute no matter how unhappy it makes you."

"Whoa. Since when have you started quoting Dolly Parton songs?"

They both laughed.

Rowena wound down first. "You really want a spell to help your guy out?"

"He's not my guy, and it's the only thing I can think of. Even if I reverse the treatments like he suggested, none would work. He's not a were so moonlight therapy's out. I doubt he'd want to go through the aversion therapy we do with vamps. After the first searing pain hit, he'd probably pass out and run like hell once he woke up. As far as the demons are concerned…uh-uh, he definitely wouldn't like what they have to go through. That only leaves magic. A potion or spell that's a one-shot deal and changes him forever to what he wants to be."

That would also get him out of the service fast. If he took treatments for months or years, as some of the clients did, that might kill her with longing.

Rowena grew thoughtful. "There is a simpler solution, you know."

"As in?"

"He can simply pretend to be a bad boy."

Becca dipped her wonton into the sweet and sour sauce. "I already suggested it. He said every time he tries, he starts to feel guilty and goes back to being nice. The poor babes—his words, not mine—get so confused, they don't know what to expect and eventually take off."

"He wants a mortal?"

"He didn't specify. My guess is mortal, immortal, anyone in between is cool with him."

"Anyone in between like you."

She tossed her untried wonton on the plate. "I didn't say that."

"But you're certain you don't want him."

Becca lied through her teeth. "Not at all."

"I'll see what I can come up with."

Chapter Four

In the stark morning light, From Crud to Stud was relatively serene. Few howls, groans or hisses sounded, no different from the streets outside. Last night's revelers were still in bed, sleeping off their hangovers. The calm had little effect on Eric's mood. What he was about to do.

A young woman at the front desk smiled sweetly at him, her outfit blinding white. He regretted having taken off his shades. "Hi, I'm Eric. I'm here for Becca. She's going to take care of me. That is, give me what I need. You know, what I should have." He chuckled. "Or rather what I have to have."

The young woman's smile had already gone kaput and her face reddened.

His had never felt hotter. "What I'm trying to say is, Becca's going to do me."

Perspiration broke out on her forehead.

His, too. For some reason, he couldn't talk like a normal person today or even a minor god with manners. "Do me for my treatment."

"Oh. Hi, I'm Heather." She beamed. "Let me buzz Becca, okay?"

"Sure. Thanks."

She leaned toward the intercom. "Hi, it's me. Sorry to bother you. I wouldn't ordinarily, but—"

"It's okay, Heather. What's up?"

His cock twitched at the question and Becca's smoky voice.

"Eric is here. For his treatment?"

"Please send him to my office."

Heather pointed her pen. "It's down that hall, first door on the left."

He already knew the location and warned himself not to race there. His feet wouldn't obey. He strode faster than he had the first time he'd been here and breezed into her private space, eager as hell to see her again. Her fragrance surrounded him, making his testosterone punch up several notches. "Hey."

She sat behind her desk, her face lowered to whatever she read, absorbed by it rather than him. "Hello."

Her frosty greeting made the temperature drop several degrees.

Eric had no idea what had caused the change in her. He was on time, actually a little early. "How've you been?"

She flipped a page. "Busy. Guess we better get to this. Pull up a chair."

With that attitude, he didn't want to. "You're going to do my treatments in here?" There wasn't any equipment around or things one might use for magic, like chicken feet, wands and other stuff.

"Before we begin, you need to read this." She slid the papers she'd been reading across the desk to him.

He grabbed a chair and sat. "Is that the process?"

"In a manner of speaking."

"What's that mean?"

"It's the contract you have to sign or nothing, and I do mean nothing, happens."

Jesus, she was hardcore today. As a rule, business owners were that way with people who didn't want their services, not ones who did. He bounced the inch-thick papers on his palm to test their weight. "I'm guessing this sucker weighs a pound. Am I right?"

She drummed her fingertips on her naked belly. Tiny silver stars cascaded from her navel. Each time she breathed, the jewelry caught the light.

He wanted to kiss the baubles and her dewy flesh.

She wore the same basic outfit she had when they had first met—flowy pants and a top that tied beneath her breasts, only these were in sapphire blue. The same shade as her eyes. Her makeup was no less dramatic than the last time—crimson lipstick that made her mouth undeniably kissable and black stuff surrounding her lids.

What a babe. Too bad she wasn't into him. Maybe with the junk she came up with to bring out his beast, she would be. "Is your service usually this complicated?" He lifted the papers and hoped she wasn't using them to run him off.

"The contract is simply full disclosure to help you understand the process. So you're completely protected."

A Wall Street hedge fund manager couldn't have sounded as evasive. "Protected against what?"

Her face paled. She gestured to the papers he held. "It's all in there. Go on, read it."

"That could take days."

She glanced to the right, the left and past him. When she'd run out of places to look, she dragged her attention back to his face. "Most of it's standard legal junk. I've highlighted the important parts."

"The ones that will release my inner beast."

"In a manner of speaking."

That again. She sounded far less confident than Eric would have liked or expected. He dropped the contract on her desk. The draft it created sent other papers floating to the edge.

Becca caught them before they fell to the floor. Her top gapped, exposing her lacy black bra.

He gripped his chair and leaned up, rubbernecking. Her bra cup dipped low, deliberately designed to expose her nipple. That baby was tight, perky and rosy. He would have bet his life her witchy fragrance and natural musk scented her skin.

His mouth watered.

She straightened and gave him an odd look. "What?"

He shouldn't have worn the stretchy boxers. His nuts could barely breathe. "Should I have a drink before I begin? Do you need one, too?"

She stopped crushing the papers in her fist. "If you've changed your mind, it's perfectly all right."

"Not a chance. What about you?"

She left her desk and crossed to the hall.

He twisted around. "Where are you going?"

"I'm just giving you space so you don't feel rushed while you read the contract."

Eric waved her back to her chair. "I'd like you to stay. You might need to explain some of this stuff to me."

She returned to her desk far slower than she'd left it. Again, she affected the pose a boss uses when prepared to terminate an employee. However, this time color stained her cheeks and her breathing grew rough.

Eric was afraid to know what in the fuck she'd come up with to help him.

He flipped through pages to the first highlighted part, read quickly and frowned. "A river bed? Fishing for frogs? Roasting them? Wearing their ashes around my neck?"

Becca cleared her throat. "In my expert opinion, the therapy we use for weres, vamps, zombies, reapers and other creatures won't work for you. Magic is the best option."

"What page in this opus does the magic stuff start on?"

She looked to the side. "Where you currently are. That's a very old spell said to work wonders on making men irresistible to women."

"No kidding. Do the people who make Axe know this? Damn, they're wasting their time on the products they put out."

Her expression darkened.

His mood went way beyond that. He yearned for the old Becca to come back. The one who'd stared at his naked junk and looked like she genuinely liked it. Where in the fuck had she gone? "I didn't say I wanted to be irresistible. I want you to release my beast."

"With that making you irresistible to women so they don't dump you, correct?"

She had a point.

"If you don't like the first spell, there are others." She inclined her head to the contract. "Keep reading."

Eric stopped halfway down the next page. "St. John's Day? When's that?"

Becca told him.

"You expect me to wait an entire year to do this?" He shook his head and read on until he got to the part about drying pigeon and blackbird brains and livers so he could sprinkle the mess on his lover's food, binding her forever to him. "Is this a joke?"

She wasn't smiling.

"You expect me to poison some poor woman with bird guts?"

"Everything in there is perfectly safe."

"You got FDA approval on it, huh?"

She looked down her nose at him. "It's merely a suggestion. Do you want those thousands of babes out there to stick with you or not?"

Call him crazy, but it sounded as though she didn't want that. Maybe that was the problem and had caused her attitude change from pleasant to nasty. Frowning, he leaned closer.

She pushed into her chair, trying to put distance between them. "What?"

He thought she might be jealous of him dating other babes, but couldn't be sure. He could always do the adult thing and ask. He'd never be that brave. If she shot him down with a hearty laugh… He didn't want to go there, which only left him pushing her damn buttons to find out what made her tick. "Yeah, I do want that. A lot."

Her jaw tightened. "Maybe it's not your niceness that's putting them off."

"Putting them off?"

"Disappointing them."

That didn't sound any better. "What's that supposed to mean?"

She peered at his fly. His ginormous erection.

Eric regarded her hard nipples.

Becca crossed her arms. If anything, that plumped her boobs. "How are you in bed?"

She couldn't be serious. "How are you?"

Her smile mocked. "This isn't about me."

"That bad, huh?"

Her grin wobbled then widened. "Don't worry—you'll never know."

Maybe that was true. Maybe it wasn't. Her snippy comment sure as hell hadn't stopped his libido from going into overdrive. If life were perfect, he'd leave his chair and trap Becca in hers, kiss her like the world was ending, haul her on the desk and love her long and hard.

Being a good guy, he remained welded to his seat. "What a shame for you to never know what I have to offer. I'm fucking great in bed."

Her expression went blurry. Her lips parted. Color rose to her throat and cheeks.

If she was trying to turn him on, she'd succeeded big time. Every muscle Eric owned shot to attention, especially the ones in his cock. Lust and excitement hardened his shaft beyond belief. Damn she was sexy and ripe as hell. All that fragrant, creamy flesh. Surely softer than a rose petal and good enough to eat, mount and screw clear into tomorrow.

If only she'd make the first move or give him a sign that he should do so.

She rolled her shoulders and shook off whatever indecent fantasy she was having. Maybe about another guy.

Disappointed, he jabbed his finger into the contract. "This is the best you can come up with. Seriously? I thought you were the head witch. You are a witch, right?"

"Are we speaking literally or figuratively?"

He fought a smile. "Literally."

Becca pushed her hair behind her ears. "Through my mom. My dad's mortal. So, no, I'm not the head witch. But I do know these are tried and true spells. However, if you prefer potions, we could go that way."

"You mean eye of newt, toe of frog, wool of bat and tongue of dog?"

"That was Shakespeare's concoction, or whoever's he plagiarized, not mine."

"What's in your potions?"

"They're my mom's. She's one-hundred-percent witch from a highly respected coven."

"Sounds good. What's she suggest?"

"The recipes start on page fifty-five."

And ended on page seventy. "This is longer than *War and Peace.*"

"You don't have to do this if you don't want to."

And miss out on their banter? Sparring with Becca was the most fun Eric had experienced in months. Hell, years. Smiling, he read the first recipe. "Red Bordeaux. Vanilla extract. Strawberry juice. Sounds like a wine cooler."

"The secret ingredients aren't spelled out."

"Why not?"

She purred. "Because they're secret."

His rod twitched at the lusty sound she'd made.

She noticed his hard-on. Her nipples peaked even more.

He liked that. "Trademarked, huh?"

"Not exactly. However, if I told you, I'd have to have Constance remove your memories."

"No need. I can live with your secrets." He pushed the contract aside. "Let's do this."

Becca regarded him intently.

Eric found her attention arousing and a bit disturbing. "What?"

"You're certain you want to go forward? There are no guarantees this will work, at least the way you think you want. It's like that old saying, 'Be careful what you wish for, you might just get it.' Once you do, there may be no going back. You'll be stuck with your new personality you think you want, even though it's not a good fit. So, are you absolutely certain?"

He wasn't any longer and had an overpowering urge to run.

Of course, it was either this or dating for eternity, especially if he couldn't screw up enough courage to ask her out or if she shot him down. That would mean going through endless other women with none working out or making him feel wanted, treasured and accepted for the long haul.

"How about you?" He clasped his hands so she wouldn't notice how they trembled. "You don't want me to do this?"

"It's not my decision."

"That's no answer."

She fiddled with her hair and her top then stroked her glinting navel stars. "I want you to be happy, Eric. Will this make you happy?"

He hadn't a clue, but her answer and her concern gave him more courage than he would have thought possible. Once his beast was released, he'd be a wild man and could find the right words and moves to woo her. "Let's find out."

She hesitated then clicked a pen and handed it to him. "Signature on the last page. Initials on pages seventeen, thirty-five, fifty-two, seventy-one and ninety-five."

Heather and Constance lingered in the hall outside Becca's office. She nodded in greeting. They glanced from the contract she held to Eric.

"Ladies." He inclined his head to them and huddled close to Becca. "They're not part of this, okay?"

His scent enveloped her. She could scarcely breathe. Her plan to be indifferent and aloof was crumbling at supersonic speed.

He spoke softly. "It's only going to be you and me, right?"

That sounded nicer than it should have. Like they were going on a date, sharing conversation, laughs, tongues, bodies, their futures. Wasn't in the cards. They were about to release something within him that probably shouldn't be set free. The damn fool was already perfect. "Yep."

"Let's do this."

Becca was beyond reluctant. She ached to tell Eric as much and kiss him until soul-deep passion kicked in. With any luck, they'd go at each other like horny teens reunited after vacation bible camp. At least in her fantasies. She dragged to the treatment room and gripped the doorknob to steady herself.

Eric pressed close. "Aren't we going in?"

They would eventually. But only because he'd insisted upon it. Wanting, or rather needing, those other babes.

She couldn't get her legs to work.

His lips grazed her ear. His breath warmed.

A delicious shiver tore through her. She longed to jump him. Maybe he wanted to do the same with her...that was why he was so close. They'd forget this spell nonsense and begin a relationship.

"Why are you hesitating?" He kept his voice low. "What exactly is in there?"

He hadn't been coming on to her. She shouldn't have been surprised or bummed. "Just stuff."

"For what?"

Weres, mainly. Even though other treatment rooms were available this morning, Becca figured this one was her best choice to conduct business, also known as her experiments, on him.

She opened the door.

He gaped at the clawed walls and the padded table. It boasted extensions for arms and legs. Leather restraints dangled from both areas. In other words, the props for an executioner's wet dream.

Eric circled the table. "You're going to strap me to this thing?"

Becca closed the door and locked it. Footfalls sounded and tapped closer, stopping at this room. She suspected Constance and Heather were out there, curious as to what was happening in there. Thankfully, there weren't closed-circuit monitors in the rooms. "The restraints are for your protection. And mine. It's in the contract." She held it up to remind him. "Page fifty-two, right above where you initialed it."

His downturned mouth said he was sorry he'd agreed to this. "How much of my beast are you going to pull out?"

"Only a little." She couldn't fuck him up too much. "If there's any at all."

"There is." He planted his hands on his lean hips. "There has to be. I'm a guy, all right?"

Becca wasn't about to argue the point. He'd worn a navy tee and battered jeans that didn't hide one muscle on his gorgeous bod. She sagged against the door, needing the support. Even his feet were luscious, nice and big. His long toes reached the edges of his leather sandals.

Given this was a weekday, he must have taken off work because he didn't know what to expect.

Neither did she and was afraid to begin. "What do you do?"

He stopped examining the wrist restraints. "Do?"

"At your job."

"Oh. I'm a financial analyst. I make sure my extended family's investments are sound. Were you thinking of investing?"

Before he whipped out his business card, Becca shook her head. "How aggressive do financial analysts get?"

"In their recommendations?"

"While they're at work. Once I've pulled out some of your inner beast, that is if there is any to pull —"

"Haven't I already said there is? Don't you worry. I don't have to be a pussycat at work." He hooked his thumbs in his front pockets. "Let's get started."

His sun-kissed locks were as mussed as they would be after he rolled off a woman and out of bed. He was wonderfully rumpled and a thousand percent male. Hotter than sin. With just a smidgen of his inner beast liberated, he'd be irresistible to every female on planet Earth and beyond.

She wanted to spit.

"Becca?"

On watery legs, she forced herself to the sink to mix the potions her mom had come up with. "Take off your clothes."

"What? Why?"

Because that's what she wanted. Today wasn't only about him. She recalled his nudity, him tugging the stretchy boxers up his powerful thighs. She wanted to see that again and would never apologize for it or confess her desire to him. "Sorry, didn't know you were modest."

"I'm not. But I am curious."

Stalling for a good lie, Becca placed the cloves and apple seeds next to the Bordeaux. "I need to see the potion's effect on every part of your body." She looked over. "All right?"

He stared at his groin. "By every part do you mean…"

"Nope. Just your skin." She hoped. If she fucked up his balls and cock… That was too terrible to consider.

He nodded agreeably and ditched his clothes. They landed on the institutional-type chairs. Naked, unashamed and well-hung, he faced her.

The world stopped.

Hard muscle draped his frame, his skin uniformly golden. No tan line. He either swam or sunbathed in the nude and was more gorgeous than any Greek or Roman god Becca had read about in her boring literature classes.

Eric scratched his hip. His balls plumped slightly. His rod was already past erect, straight to rock hard.

She wasn't certain if he was turned on by her or simply showing off. Probably the latter. Guys were super sensitive about how long they were and their sexual prowess.

"Becca?"

"Huh?"

"What happens now?"

Not what she wanted, that was for sure. "Turn around."

He frowned. "Why?"

So she'd quit picturing herself on her knees, his glorious shaft and balls in her palms and mouth. "I can't let you see the secret ingredients I'm using."

"Would I even recognize them?"

"You might."

"Then they're normal."

"Define normal."

"Oh, hey." He crossed the room. His cock bounced with each step. "You're not using bird guts, are you?"

Enthralled with how his male equipment pointed at her, she needed a moment to understand his question. "No. Just herbs and stuff."

"What kind of stuff?"

His crown had bypassed crimson and was now maroon with arousal, the skin stretched so much it shone. She wished she was the cause. Since she wasn't, she hated her foolish desire and self-indulgence in staring at him. Damn, when would she ever learn? "Stuff you buy in a regular grocery store. Stuff you've eaten. Stuff mortals have eaten. Now, I mean it, dammit. Turn. Around."

He backed away from her snarl. The padded table stopped him. He rubbed his bumped ass and birthmark.

Becca figured that's why he had insisted on facing her. He didn't want her looking at or making fun of what he considered a fatal flaw. She wouldn't. Though she might lick it several times. "If you refuse to turn around, at least close your eyes."

He rolled them first, then on a frustrated huff, he obeyed her.

Becca locked her knees to stay put. If she got any nearer to him, she'd lick his prominent Adam's apple and bristly chin then tongue his tiny nipples. Beneath his half-moon navel, dark hairs trickled to his groin. More hair dusted his muscular thighs and calves.

He put Michelangelo's David to shame. No artist, however talented, could have captured Eric's male beauty.

He shifted his weight. His rod swung to the right and left, like a carnal pendulum. "How long will it take you to mix that stuff?"

All day and night, if Becca had her way, which she didn't. "Bored already?"

"Nope. You?"

He had to know how she stared at him and lusted after his perfect bod, wicked humor and kind heart. That made her the first of the next million women who'd want him. She lowered her face and nursed her bruised and needy heart. "I'll be through in no time at all."

"Just tell me when I can open my eyes."

Not even a cattle prod could have prompted her to rush. To keep him from suspecting as much, she slid bottles around to create a mild racket. His muscular biceps enchanted her. So, did his impressive forearms. She counted his abs. He had a mole on his upper left thigh and faint freckles on his shoulders.

Becca would have given several years of her life to touch them. At the very least, she should have taken his picture with her smartphone. Too late now unless she conjured the device from her desk. With her lousy magic, she might hit her chair instead, reducing it to pieces or dust. Maybe her mom was right about magic knowing when it wasn't respected or wanted. If Becca had desired it as much as she did Eric, she'd rule the sorcerer world.

Irresistibly, he drew her closer, his heat and male appeal a lure she couldn't resist. "I'm done."

He started.

She was almost on top of him, close enough to kiss. Before he freaked out, she stepped around to the treatment table and patted it. "Hop on."

He climbed on to the buttery leather. "You know, I've had dreams like this."

"Being treated for your affliction?"

His smile faded. "Being taken advantage of by a woman."

Against her better judgment, she ran her thumbnail up his hairy calf.

He grunted appreciatively. His balls contracted and pressed into his groin.

If she hadn't been trying to maintain her dignity, she would have squealed in delight. "Being taken advantage of isn't in your contract."

Eric sighed. His pecs trembled. "It should be."

She lowered her face to hide her grin. "Go on, lie down. I won't hurt you."

"It's okay if you do. I'm kind of liking this."

Her pulse jumped at his comment. She stared at his eyes.

He blinked. "What?"

She couldn't tell if he was merely making conversation or if he meant what he'd said. "Nothing." She put his wrists and ankles into the restraints and tightened them.

His love affair with bondage ended, a frown replacing his dopey look. He squeezed his fists and yanked against the leather, trying to break free.

"Careful." She stroked an old scar on his knee, possibly from a childhood accident. Even the whitish skin was beautiful. "You're going to hurt yourself."

"More than you have? I'm trying to keep the circulation going that you cut off. These are restraints not tourniquets. Loosen them up please."

"No." Becca didn't trust herself while he was free. "They're perfect." She strolled to the sink and returned with a champagne flute. "Drink this."

"That's the potion?"

"Yep."

He arched one eyebrow. "You serve it to all your clients in a flute?"

"You're the first. If you were a were, I'd probably put it in a doggy bowl for you to lap up. A vamp might get it intravenously. Since you don't seem to like surgery or anything involving pain, I decided to put it in a glass. Go on. Sip."

Becca cupped his head and lifted it to help him take a drink.

He made a face first then dipped his tongue into the liquid and smacked his lips. Delight registered in his eyes. "Not bad. Reminds me of pink lemonade."

It shouldn't have. Becca frowned at the glass and looked over. "Hold on. This is my Crystal Light. Be right back."

She pushed the real potion at him. "Drink. It won't be so bad."

"Hold my nose for me?"

"Sure."

He gulped a mouthful and gagged. "Aw, shit. What happened to the wine cooler in the contract? This crap is worse than sucking on dirty socks."

"No pain, no gain. Go on. Just one more sip."

He turned his face away. "Why only one?"

"We better take this slow."

Eric regarded his spread-eagled bod, restraints and nudity. "Little late for that, wouldn't you say?"

She snickered then growled. "Drink."

"Only for you." He scrunched his face, took a sip and heaved air as the formerly dead do when they'd been shocked back to life.

Becca released his head. "Relax."

"I'm trying. I can't. Is it working?"

"It's only been a second. You're just scared."

"Oh hey, I'm never—" His eyes goggled at something only he could see or feel.

Her stomach clenched. "Eric?"

His lids slid down and his head fell to one side.

Bile rose to her throat. "Hey."

He didn't respond.

Holy fuck, she'd killed him. Or rather her mother had with her potion. "Oh, my God, Eric. Talk to me, please."

"Becca!" Constance pounded on the door. "Everything okay?"

Heather cried out, "You want us to call someone?"

Becca hadn't a clue who that might be. 9-1-1 for Immortals? Heather was the healer here, but she'd never worked on a Roman god before. She could mess him up even more than he already was. "Everything's fine. Stay out there. Do not unlock the door and come inside."

"Eric?" She shook his shoulders. His hands flopped, the same as a ragdoll does. She ran her nail up his inner legs. Nada. His cock was fucking flaccid, but still long and gorgeous. "Eric, please. Oh, crap, wake—"

He laughed. "Had you there, didn't I—? Ow."

She smacked his shoulder again.

"Damn." He tried to pull away from her. The restraints stopped him. "That hurts."

"Oh, yeah? Good."

He met her glare with his own. "When are you going to be nice to me?"

Becca stepped back. Real pain, the emotional kind, flooded his face. Couldn't be from the potion. It was supposed to release his beast, not tender needs. Ones as great as her own.

Not knowing what to think, she went with her gut and ran her fingers through his thick, silky hair. "Sorry. I didn't mean to snap at you."

He smiled. "It's okay."

"No, it's not." He was being too nice again. Not that she minded, but he would and might want his entire beast unleashed. Something that would totally screw him up.

"You didn't mean to treat me badly. You're doing great now massaging my scalp." He winked. "Don't stop."

Becca brought back her hand. His hair stuck to it. While his head…

She gasped.

"What?" He tried to see what she had but couldn't. "What?"

Clumps of his hair fell from her fingers. Worse, thicker, darker hair, similar to a gorilla's, sprouted on his pecs, torso and belly.

That, he saw. "Oh, holy shit."

Becca yanked open the door and shrieked, "Zoe!"

"Why in the fuck are you calling her?" His fists and feet pounded the table. He yanked on his restraints.

"Calm down. I'm not doing this to hurt you."

He moaned. "You already have."

Her heart pounded. "Zoe."

She shot out of a treatment room. "Yo. What's wrong?"

"I need my smartphone. It's on my desk."

"On it." She bolted down the hall.

"No—stop! I don't have time for you to get it that way. Use your dark powers."

Eric gasped. "Why the fuck do you want her to do that?"

"To get my phone."

Zoe frowned. "You know I can't use them. I'm trying to be good." She gestured helplessly. "Like a mortal. Doing things the hard way no matter how painful that may—"

"Okay, okay, okay." Becca didn't have time for this. "Go. Get it off my desk the usual way and bring it to me."

She sped away.

Eric's fists rammed into the table. "Who are you going to call? Please, not my uncle. I left him as my emergency contact on the contract. If he sees me like this, he'll never let me live it down. You can't call him."

"Relax, I'm not. I'm going to phone my mom. She'll help. She'll stop whatever's wrong with the potion."

"How can you be so sure?"

"Like I already told you, she's the one who came up with them."

"And you want her to do worse than this?" he wailed.

Zoe rounded the corner at a run and skidded down the hall. "Here." She threw the phone.

Becca caught it. "Thanks." She shut and locked the door, called her mom and explained the problem. "This has to be fixable." She spoke mega-low. "Please tell me it is."

Eric cried out. "Oh, fuck. Oh, holy shit."

Rowena clucked her tongue. "Is that your Roman god? Does he always talk like that?"

Becca wanted to die. She spoke through her teeth. "He's upset, Mom. He has a right to be. His head is already bald and the rest of him is…" She couldn't say it. Thick, shaggy hair was still budding from Eric's ears, nostrils and soles. Every-freaking-where it shouldn't be. "You said this would work."

"I said it might. Are you taking this magic seriously, as I advised?"

"Would I be screaming at you and begging if I weren't? What's it matter, anyway, how dedicated I am with this? It's a potion, not a spell. You said my conjuring didn't work because I couldn't care less about it. This potion should be fine on its own no matter how bored I am with magic, right?"

"As a rule. Clearly, him being a god is different than if he was a demon, vampire or a warlock."

"You think?"

"Becca, I'm trying to help, all right? No reason to get snotty."

She held back a screech. "Tell me what to do. What's the antidote? Holy shit, there is an antidote, isn't there?"

"Oh, fuck." Eric groaned.

Rowena sniffed. "You two need to clean up your language."

"Mom. This. Is. Freaking Serious. All right?"

"Okay, okay. Let me think."

Seconds crawled by. Eric groaned, growled and swore. Hair sprouted in tuffs on his palms and elsewhere.

"Mom, you better hurry." Becca bounced in place. "His lips and tongue are getting hairy. What are we going to do? Are you still there?"

"Of course, I am. I'm thinking."

"Don't take too long. We have to get him back to the way he was when he first came in here. He can't leave looking like this." She lowered her voice even more. "He can barely speak."

Gagging sounds poured from him. He swore. The hair in his mouth muffled what he'd said.

"Mom?"

"I'm trying my best. Please tell me you had him sign the contract before you gave him anything."

Becca ground her fist into her forehead. "Why are you asking?"

"Just wanted to be certain, that's all. Try this."

"Wait." She grabbed a pen and notepad to write down the potion. "Go on."

Rowena told her what she needed.

"You're sure?" If this got any worse for Eric… "Tell me you're totally sure."

"I'm relatively so."

Nauseous, Becca scribbled the last ingredient. "Got it. Bye." She spoke to Eric. "Give me a sec to mix the stuff."

"You mean another potion from your mom?" He coughed and spit out hair wads. "Isn't there anyone else you could call?"

"She's the best."

"Oh, dear God." He battled against the restraints. They won. Panting, he dropped his head to the cushion. "What if your new potion kills me? Shit, shit, shit. That may be the only way to fix this."

"Stop talking like that. Gods can't be killed." At least as far as Becca knew. However, she was no expert. "You're going to be fine."

Her hands shook so much she dropped two containers and spilled the contents of the third.

Eric thrashed. He cursed. He spit up more hair.

"Here." She held up his head as she had before. "Only a sip."

He tried to guzzle it.

"Hey, not so much."

"What else could it do to me?"

Becca tried to picture him as a woman. A tall, muscular, ugly woman. She pushed the image away and prayed that horrible transformation wouldn't happen.

She put the flute aside and held his hand.

He curled his fingers over hers. "Don't let go. Please."

"I won't. I'll be here until this…" She forgot what she'd intended to say.

He cringed. "What's it doing now? Don't keep it from me. I have to know. No, I don't want to."

"It's okay. Really. You're back." Amazingly so.

He stared at her then what he could see of himself. His pecs and torso were all caramel-colored skin again. His palms, soles, lips and tongue as hairless as they'd been before.

Eric looked upward, straining to see his hair. "What's happening on my head?"

"You look the same as you did when you came in."

He collapsed and gulped air. "Thanks — wait. What about my junk?" He craned his neck to see. "Did anything happen to it? Aw shit, not that."

"Take it easy. It looks fine."

"Does it work?" Panic whisked across his face. "I don't think it's working."

"Hang on." Becca released his hand and leaned down to his cock. "I think it's bigger."

He grinned then went pale. "What if it's bloated because it's dead?"

"It's not dead." Becca stroked his shaft. It blossomed faster than a morning glory responding to the sun. In seconds, his erection was impressive as all hell. Thick. Hard. Macho-man virile. "It's definitely okay."

To make sure, she fondled him and trembled at his rod's musky scent.

Eric grunted. A coarse, masculine sound. His toes curled and his fingers fisted. He growled. "Come here."

She played with his crown and drew her fingertip across the satiny skin to the bumpier part in back. Next, she touched the tiny slit. Pre-cum glistened on it.

"Becca."

"Uh-huh."

"Come. Here."

His command brooked no argument. It was bad boy through and through. Possibly from the second potion, the first or them combined. Or maybe from her fondling his cock. Becca couldn't stop. She stroked his crown. "What?"

"I said now. Right this minute."

She obeyed him more than she'd done with any man. He oozed naked lust and intolerable desire. "Are you feeling all right?"

His nostrils flared slightly. His irises darkened from hazel to deep chocolate brown.

He wasn't okay. At least the okay he'd been before the last potion. Meaning, nice and polite. This was the new Eric.

His raw magnetism transfixed her.

He made a low noise. A male calling to a female. "Closer."

She did as he demanded. Their sighs mingled.

"No." A feral emotion sparked in his eyes. "Closer."

Her lips brushed his.

He yanked his restraints.

Becca kept him her prisoner. She cupped his bristly cheek and slipped her tongue into his awesome mouth. The sun couldn't have been hotter. The Gulf wetter. Her legs bowed. He tasted clean, sweet and completely male.

On a shameless groan, he pushed her tongue aside and filled her mouth instead.

Even chocolate-covered diamonds wouldn't have matched this gift. She sucked his tongue and explored his sculptured abs and the thick hair on his groin.

He lifted his hips, offering himself to her.

She'd be a fool not to accept. More pre-cum seeped from the small fissure in his crown, verifying his passion for her, no one else. She shivered in delight.

He pulled his mouth free. "Take off your clothes."

Not certain she'd heard him correctly, she eased back. "What?"

"Strip. Now." Aching desire filled his eyes. "You're too far away. You're wearing too many damn clothes." He battled his restraints. "Why are you torturing me?"

He was doing that to her. Never had she wanted a guy as she did him and this was certainly her only chance to get close, at least physically. That, alone, should have had her begging off to avoid future heartache.

"Come on, come on, come on." He grimaced. "Don't make me wait any longer. I have to smell you again. Touch you and taste you."

"Eric, are you all right?"

"Hell, no." His face was the same shade as her lipstick. "I want you, dammit."

He did. Never had she witnessed a man in more carnal pain around her.

She tore at her clothes and ripped the ties on her top to remove the stupid thing. Her harem pants snagged on her sandals.

"No. The heels stay on." He grinned lewdly. "So does the jewelry. Lose the bra and thong."

She obeyed, unable to consider anything except the next few seconds or hopefully minutes.

Eric's smile was beyond depraved, promising damnation and heaven with each kiss, lick and fuck.

"Get me out of these things." He tugged on the leather restraints.

"No."

He gaped. "You can't keep me tied up."

"You're not tied. You're buckled. Now keep quiet."

"No fucking way. I said to… What are you doing?"

"What do you think?" She climbed on the table with an ease that said it was the most natural thing to do in a public business. Her cunt faced him. His precious package lay mere inches beneath her lips.

He smelled of life, a male beast, a man she liked, even though she shouldn't. Refusing to think about the downside after this ended, she went for broke. "Bon appétit."

Becca rubbed her nose against his hairy groin, wanting his scent on her. Musk had never smelled more decadent or fabulous. Next, she eased his cock aside and licked his balls.

He stiffened and let out a bawdy cry.

A fist rapped on the door, the knock light and uncertain. Sounded like something Heather might do.

Becca ignored it.

The meagre tapping resumed. "Are you all right in there?"

Eric growled, "Go away."

"Heather, please." Becca begged as she never had. "Don't come in."

"Okay. I'm sorry. I shouldn't have bothered you. I won't do so again. I just thought – "

Eric's wild moan drowned out Heather's unending apology.

Becca would have smiled, but she was too busy easing his right ball into her mouth. His skin was hot and slightly salty.

He made joyful sounds and noises Becca had never heard before, maybe Roman god talk. Who knew?

Before she could ask, he pulled himself together and licked her cunt.

Her tongue stalled on his sac.

With impressive skill, he held her clit between his teeth and lapped it mercilessly.

Warmth pooled in her groin and thighs. Civilization fell away, allowing Becca to revert to her animal nature, wanting nothing except to savor her hedonistic core. She slipped his cock into her mouth tonsil-deep. Her chin touched his thick pelt, fragrant from his scent. Gently, she fondled his balls.

He wasn't as delicate with her clit. He licked, sucked and claimed it ruthlessly.

Her knees shook. Her bod felt too heavy to keep up. Even so, she fought climax, never wanting this to end.

Eric didn't come, either. He tensed his legs and curled his toes a lot.

She suspected he was battling his inner urges.

Bad boy that he was, he tongued the area around her nub then unexpectedly tongued her clit.

She jerked.

He abandoned her most sensitive spot and licked her cleft.

Nice, but she liked the other stuff better.

He returned to her nub and went at it relentlessly, his actions keeping her off-guard.

Making her needy and wanting.

Perspiration clung to her. She was close to collapse but delivered herself to him and came on an explosive gasp.

His piercing shout signaled his release.

Cum spurted into her mouth. Still struggling for air, she drank his creamy offering, loving its flavor, so different from the warlocks, demons and weres she'd hooked up with.

They were mere immortals.

She'd just tasted ambrosia from a god. Eric was that. Perfect in every way. Especially now. Aided by the second potion, the first had worked as it should and released just enough beast. The best part.

He heaved air, coughed and quieted down.

She should have welcomed the silence and a chance to cuddle but couldn't. Sated and relaxed, he might want to talk about stuff. Like the babes he could snare now since he was no longer Mr. Nice Guy.

Becca's sexual hangover hit faster than she'd dreamed possible. She felt horribly naked and downright foolish. The same as in middle school when she'd screwed up enough courage to ask a less-than-cool guy to the homecoming dance, a huge deal. He'd said yes then canceled two days before the event when a cuter girl asked him to go with her. The remaining school year had been purely awful. She'd run into him constantly. He'd never looked her way. He'd saved his attention and affection for the other girl.

That wasn't something Becca intended to repeat with Eric.

He yawned.

With any luck, he'd conk out as most guys did after sex.

Hoping for that, she crawled off him and the table, grabbed her clothes and held them over her nudity.

Eric went from sleepy to alert in a second. "What are you doing?"

"Leaving. Go on, get dressed. You can take off, too."

"Are you kidding?"

"The second potion worked."

"Yeah, I know." He sat up. The restraints pulled him back.

She'd forgotten about them. "Give me a sec." With one arm holding her clothes to her boobs, she unbuckled his right wrist. "There." She skittered back. "You can get the others yourself."

"What's wrong?"

"Nothing. I have work to do."

He glanced at her cunt, exposed beneath her clothes and still wet from his tongue. "Now?"

"Yeah. Glad the potion worked. You did good." She gave him a thumbs-up and escaped into the hall, not considering what her staff might think about her being naked or what had just happened with him.

Becca simply needed to flee her feelings for Eric.

Chapter Five

Talk about being treated like a piece of meat.

I did good?

As opposed to what? Something that would have kept Becca on top of him, indulging in her X-rated fantasies, loving his balls and cock?

That wasn't going to happen now and Eric hadn't a clue why. He'd behaved like the badass he'd always wanted to be, ordering her around and demanding she strip. She'd had no problem with that or him gorging on her slick pussy. Hell, he'd sucked her rigid little clit with far more than finesse. He'd adored it with damn need and drove her wild. He'd lifted his hips so she could play with his nuts.

That had been so fucking sweet. His ears had buzzed from her tongue rasping against his sac, her mouth heating his balls and her nub growing harder with his licks. Her scent still invaded this room and his senses, turning his legs to jelly.

What they'd shared had been damn nice. No, it had been pissing great. Yet here he was nude, used and abused and fighting the leather restraint on his wrist while she was in the hall, consoling Heather, not him.

"I'm all right, really." Becca's voice trembled. "Never been better."

Heather made a pained sound. "But you're naked."

"Look, I'm getting dressed."

"Did he attack you and rip off your clothes?"

He was horny, not Houdini. The stupid restraints wouldn't budge.

Becca sighed loudly. "It's complicated."

At last, she'd got something right about how she'd treated him.

Heather whimpered.

"Hey, everything's cool." Becca chuckled. "Okay?"

It wasn't anywhere near that for Eric. He longed to see Becca's plush ass, lavish breasts and every other damned inch on her glorious bod for as long as he wanted. The same as what she'd done with him, insisting he undress, screaming at him to keep his eyes closed while she mixed that shitty-tasting potion.

Secret ingredients, his butt.

He hadn't been born yesterday in a literal or figurative sense. Becca had wanted a chance to stare at his stuff. What normal guy would argue with that? Not him. He gave her exactly what she craved. If anything, that made him accommodating to a fault. The problem that had brought him here.

No more. He was through with being polite.

"Oh, no." Heather inhaled sharply. "Your top's torn."

"Not that much. See? The ties still work."

"But it's ripped. Did he do that?"

Eric made a face. Heather said 'he' like it was a four-letter word.

"No." Becca cleared her throat. "I did."

"Oh, okay. But why would you do that?"

Because she couldn't strip and crawl on me fast enough. That had been pure magic. No way did he believe she behaved that way with her other clients.

Unless she did.

Doubt crept in. On a muttered curse, he shoved it away. It pushed back. Misgiving flooded his brain.

She'd downed the liquid in her champagne flute, claiming it was Crystal Light. It was always possible she'd added something that made her horny so she'd be stoked for sex. Eric couldn't figure out why she'd have to prepare for that, unless he wasn't enough for her as he was and she'd put a clause in his contract about them doing the nasty.

She'd left the papers near the sink.

He freed his wrist and ankles then left the table fast and lost his balance. His legs and ass thudded on the floor.

Heather squeaked. "What was that?"

"Nothing. Go back to work." Becca rapped on the door. "You okay in there?"

You, not babe or even Eric. As though he was a complete stranger even after the monumental orgasms they'd given each other. "What do you think?"

Her heels stopped clicking on the floor. "Do you need any help?"

If she meant from her weirdo staff, then the answer was no. It seemed unlikely Becca would offer him a hand, boob, nipple, clit or anything else he wanted. "Nope. I'm great. Just like you promised in the contract. Page seventy-three, I believe. Right below my initials."

She tapped her foot. The sound matched the noise a pointer made when hitting a teacher's palm before she swung the thing at a mouthy student. "Well, good then."

Eric caught the "screw you" behind her words. She'd already done that to him by running from the room.

"It's what you wanted." Her accusation poured through the door. "Heather will get you a receipt. Have a great day."

Becca hurried down the hall, heels tapping, leaving him alone, dismissed and forgotten.

Eric rubbed his battered ass and padded to his contract. Nowhere in the thing was there a clause about her having sex with him for treatment purposes or for any other reason.

She'd wanted him then she hadn't, then she'd got pissed about it. Like it was his fault she couldn't get away from him fast enough. No different from every other woman in his life, which put him right back to where he started.

Except this time, he intended to find out why.

Becca faced her office window. Tourists strolled past on the street below. Mainly families with little kids who jumped rather than walked. Their tiny voices squealed. They pointed at stuff they wanted their parents to buy. Junk that would make them happy.

She tried to recall when life had been that simple. A time when it didn't matter if a little girl wasn't beautiful and slender, or if a boy didn't measure up to whatever society dictated for a male. Moments when being alive, healthy and ready for anything was good enough.

Then puberty kicked in and screwed everything up, replacing inexhaustible wonder and confidence with endless uncertainty.

Eric had said he was great. The potion had worked. He'd been so eager to get out of there and test his new personality he'd fallen off the table.

She wrapped her arms around herself. Maybe he'd want another potion to make him less klutzy. If he did, she was going to let Zoe give it to him. In more ways than one.

Becca leaned against the window and fingered the safety pin holding her torn ties together. Proof she'd behaved idiotically. The blouse was ruined. She'd have to pitch the damn thing.

No way would she keep it as a memento of her one passionate encounter with Eric. She'd stopped being sentimental during her sophomore year in high school when she'd planned to save the football program as a keepsake to commemorate the one game she'd gone to with a guy, a fix-up from another school. She'd tried to dazzle him with her sports knowledge. Becca's dad had drilled her for weeks about each play. Like a trained seal, she'd performed beautifully that afternoon.

Her date had rewarded her with a pat on her shoulder, the kind reserved for a buddy or faithful dog. No kiss had followed. He'd taken off as quickly as he could, never to be seen again.

Becca was through with that shit. She rubbed her temple.

Her door flew open and smacked into a potted fern.

Eric closed the door, righted the plant and tried to fluff its bent fronds.

"That's okay." She held up her hand before he made things worse. "I'll get it."

He dropped the frond he'd broken off. Shoulders squared, he faced her. "We need to talk."

She rounded her desk, her finger poised above the intercom button. "I'll have Zoe in here in a minute."

"Won't do any good." He stalked to Becca's desk, his fist around the contract. "I'm not leaving until you and I talk even if Zoe does go a couple rounds with me. She can fry the hair off my balls if she wants, but I don't hurt women. They do that to me."

Becca stepped back. "I thought she could quote you a price for our potions and spells if you wanted something else now."

"Like what?" His eyes shot up as they had when he'd been strapped to the table. He patted his head. "Is my hair falling out again?"

"It's fine." Tousled and perfect.

"Then why would I need another potion?"

Her cheeks got hot. "You fell off the table in the treatment room. You messed up my plant. We can give you something to make you..." She searched for the right words that wouldn't piss him off further but couldn't find any.

"Let me help." He crossed his arms. "Something to make me less clumsy?"

"More graceful."

"Just what I want, to move like a ballet dancer. That ought to make me a real babe magnet."

Becca couldn't believe this. The only thing on his damn mind was his stupid conquests. She clenched her jaw. "I'm only trying to help."

He dropped his contract on her desk, pulled his AmEx from his wallet and tossed the card to her.

It hit her boob.

He stared at her mega-tight nipples. "Sorry for being so clumsy."

Didn't sound like it to her.

He gestured to the card. "Fill that up for all I care. Just don't call Zoe or anyone else in here. I don't want to be bent, folded or mutilated any longer. I'm tired of getting hurt."

Second time he'd said that. Unhappiness registered beneath his new nasty attitude and irritation. "Is the potion wearing off?"

It was supposed to be permanent, unless her mom had diluted the ingredients, afraid they'd cause some other weird reaction.

"I don't know." He examined himself, maybe looking for hair sprouting or different flaws. "Do you?"

His uncertainty touched Becca as few things had. She wanted to pull him into her embrace and reassure him, but couldn't. She wasn't that courageous or controlled. If he ordered her to undress again, she'd do so gladly, would lie on her desk and invite him to do smutty things to her, which she'd regret later.

Best to keep her distance. "How do you feel?"

"Bruised and used. I did good in there?" He flung his arm in the general direction of the treatment room. "Are you kidding me?"

Becca wasn't certain what he wanted her to say or whether this was the real Eric talking. Could be the potion urged him on. She fingered her torn top. "Don't you think you did good?"

He strode around her desk.

She retreated.

He followed and pointed at her. "You're not turning this around on me. Are you actually saying you didn't enjoy what we did?"

Ah, this was about her reaction to him. She fled her feelings and his proximity. A chair to the side blocked her. She rushed around it.

Eric pursued.

"Of course, I enjoyed it." At this point, confession was her only option. She halted. "Didn't you hear the noises I made?"

"I was too busy making my own. However, mine were real. Men can't fake orgasms."

"You think I faked that?"

"I don't know. You tell me." He pulled up a chair and sat. "Go on."

Becca leaned against her desk and stalled for the right thing to say. Something that would convince him what a stud he was, which wasn't a lie, while also avoiding how much she foolishly wanted him. Doing that would leave her dignity intact. A win-win for them both.

Eric planted his hands on his knees and leaned forward. "I'm waiting, Becca."

She pulled a loose thread on her ties. The tear in them widened beneath the safety pin. "What we did was wonderful. I wasn't faking. I don't do that."

Something crossed his face that she couldn't read.

He pushed it aside and doubled down on his piercing look, the kind TV cops use during interrogations. "Why did you do it at all? It's not in the contract." He gestured to the papers. "I know. I finally read the dumb thing."

Becca gestured helplessly, her cheeks burning.

"Sorry, but I can't read sign language. You're going to have to tell me."

Running like hell seemed a better option until he caught up with her, which he would, given his new assertive personality. "Why?"

"Because I want to know. Why did you do it, Becca? Exactly, precisely, explicitly why?"

"I got caught up in the moment, all right? Same as you."

A muscle in his jaw jumped. "And that's all it was."

Not even close. However, Becca wasn't a schoolgirl any longer, wanting what she couldn't have — being noticed, liked, loved. "Isn't that enough?"

He glanced past her to hazy sun streaming through the windows. The light turned his skin a paler gold and lightened the blond streaks in his hair, making him look like an unearthly vision of the perfect man. In other words, irresistible. Precisely what he'd asked for when he hadn't needed a makeover to begin with.

A new emotion touched his eyes. He repressed it quickly before she could interpret it. "I don't know if the potion's still working on me or not. Guess I'll have to test it out."

Of course, he would. Poor guy didn't have any other choice, except to surround himself with adoring babes. Becca plodded around her desk. "Have fun."

"I intend to."

Envy and sorrow tore through her, stealing her breath. To hide her pain, she made a great show of writing down his AmEx number, expiration date and the codes, which Heather already had, then extended the card to him. "We'll keep your information on file if you need additional treatments."

"Thanks." He slipped the card into his wallet.

"If they don't work, we'll refund you fully." A promise she made all clients. Eric wasn't special. He was merely a customer she'd never see again. Her heart ached worse than before. "It's only fair. You can use what you paid us to get behavior modification from a licensed psychologist or psychiatrist. Maybe that's your best bet. Doing things the mortal way."

She forced a smile.

He didn't return it. His silence grew. His focus on her never wavered.

Embarrassment and desire battled within her. She'd never sweated so much in her life and didn't know what else she could offer him or what he could possibly want. She, and her mom, had tried their best with the potions. Becca had celebrated their eventual success by giving him head and admitting she enjoyed it. Hell, she'd even torn her blouse. Talk about enthusiasm. "I know you're upset."

"You don't know me at all."

That hurt deep and hard. Her blush didn't help, humiliating her further. Of course, she didn't know him, nor would she. That wasn't in their futures. However, it didn't take a psychic or a trained shrink to see he wasn't happy. She cleared her throat, avoided his gaze and tried to comfort. "I want you to know that should you return for additional services, we'll do everything we can to see that you succeed at what you came for."

"Yes, you will. But I'm not waiting for that. Be ready at nine tonight."

She stopped writing his description next to the credit card number, her adjectives pornographic. She rested her fist on them. "You want another appointment this evening?"

"I want to test out the lasting effects of the potion."

"We don't have any way to measure that here. You're a first."

"Lucky me." He lost his smile. "Not here. At a restaurant."

Becca wasn't following then she was. Her sorrow turned to quick outrage. "You want me to follow you to a restaurant and watch how you're behaving with another woman?"

"Not at all. I want you to be that woman."

His answer caught her off guard. She sank to her chair. "Like a date?"

"Call it a test run." He watched her closely. The way a man does when he's gauging a woman's reaction to him.

Becca had already passed that test when she'd worshipped his cock. "A test run."

"Isn't that enough?"

He'd parroted her earlier words.

Her answer was simple. What he proposed wasn't enough, though it might be a start. No, that was nuts. He was nothing more than a client. Once he had his new personality down pat, he'd forget her in a moment. There were too many distractions in life—blondes, brunettes, other redheads.

In here, he noticed her alone, his attention riveted.

Becca wasn't certain why and figured she should ask her mom if his current behavior was potion-related. "Ah…"

"No, ahs, ifs, ands or buts. I'll pick you up at your place. Nine tonight."

Sounded good to her. "No."

"You're refusing me?"

She had no choice and would continue to do so if she had any sense. Unfortunately, using logic had never been her greatest strength when it came to men. Even after she'd locked her heart away when she'd dated weres, vamps and warlocks, she'd still pined for more. Hopelessly. Endlessly. "You can pick me up here, at the office—no, wait."

She didn't want Heather, Constance, Zoe or the twins to know what was going on. It was bad enough when a guy dumped her. Suffering through her friends' and staff's condolences only prolonged the agony. "I'll meet you there. Wherever there is."

A slow, sexy smile spread across his face. "We could forget the restaurant and eat at my place."

Heat pooled in Becca's groin, waking up her pussy, priming it for his cock.

"That way we won't be disturbed." He winked. "Just you, me and the effects of the potion."

Yeah, the potion. Magic. Not the real Eric yearning for her. "No."

He made a face. "Look, I'll be a perfect gentleman." He grinned slyly. "Within reason."

There wasn't anything reasonable about this. "No. A restaurant or nothing."

On an exasperated sigh, he sagged in his chair. "Italian? French? Cajun? Chinese? Japanese? Come on. Help me out here. Don't make me go through every ethnic variation. You do eat food, right? I mean, witches don't have a special menu I'm unaware of, like lizard's legs and howlet's wing."

Shakespeare again. "Relax. I've been known to eat a Whopper every now and then."

"You certainly did."

The yummy bulge behind his fly bulked up quickly. No different from when she'd excited him with her mouth. "You better start measuring that." She inclined her head to his cock. "Since you drank the potion, it seems to be getting bigger."

"As long as it doesn't trip me while I walk, I'm good."

She ran her finger around her doodles that depicted his lovely balls and rod. "But think of the poor women."

"Oh, yeah. There is that. Do well-endowed men bother you, Becca?"

Nothing about him disturbed her in the least, except whether this was the way he flirted or if the potion was talking for him. Becca still wasn't certain. If his personality was now magic-related, she'd be disappointed. If this was the real Eric letting loose and having fun, she'd probably fall in love. What a bummer. "Italian."

"Well-endowed Italian men bother you. Wow, that's a surprise. In the treatment room, I could have sworn—"

"That's my choice for food tonight." Her nipples were so hard they stung.

Eric's attention dipped from her mouth to her breasts. "Italian, huh? That's what you want?"

Yep. They both knew they weren't talking about food.

Chapter Six

If it wouldn't have made him look like a total loon, Eric would have boogied out of Becca's building. Whether his exuberance was related to the potion, her effect on him or their promising night together, he didn't know or care.

Intoxicated from something indescribable, not exactly hope or lust, but a delirious combination of the two, he smiled at the annoying tourists, their screeching kids and the other crap that usually kept him away from the French Quarter. Even the soupy air embraced him as it never had.

Sweating worse than Mitt Romney during his presidential debates, Eric wove through the crowd and brought up the address book on his smartphone.

His call connected on the second ring. He spoke first. "Hey. Is that you, Uncle Desi?" Short for Desiderio. Italian for desire.

A snort answered. "Hey, yourself. Is that you, Eros?"

His cheeks got hot enough to roast marshmallows. If the second potion hadn't fixed him and Heather had

Tina Donahue

been forced to call Desi, his emergency contact, Eric wouldn't have been a dead man...he would have simply wished he were. He crossed the street to the obnoxious families on that side and kept his voice low. "It's Eric, please."

"You young people." He made a derisive noise.

Eric suspected Desi had also raised his eyes to Mount Olympus, aka heaven for them, and the family's distant relatives there — Zeus, Hera and Poseidon. Deities their ancestors appropriated from the Greeks then renamed Jupiter, Juno and Neptune. Godly plagiarism. "Can you reserve a table for me tonight?"

Desi's Italian restaurant was the best in New Orleans. Unfortunately.

"Of course. You even have to ask?"

"One of the more private tables, if you can."

"Ah, I see now. Another woman. Don't you never intend to settle down and start a family? Have you forgotten your heritage?"

Eric should be so lucky. He cupped his phone close to his mouth so the passing tourists wouldn't overhear his conversation and call the mental health department to have him locked up. "It's not like I can shoot the ladies with an arrow, Uncle Desi. That went out with Zeus catting around on Hera. Women don't put up with that crap any longer. They want — hell, I don't know what they want — but if I shot anything at a woman, she'd have me arrested for assault with a deadly weapon. And rightfully so."

Desi muttered beneath his breath.

Eric shrugged. "It's a different world."

"Bullshit. It's never changed. You young people have, and not for the best."

"Sorry, but I have to do this my way."

"You mean, like a mortal."

Eric thought about the potions he'd sipped, his meltdown in Becca's treatment room, her cunt above his face and his cock in her mouth. That was pure magic. "Powers don't always work the way we want."

"Tell that to Jupiter. He'd be surprised."

Having reached his Mercedes, Eric dropped into the front seat and turned the air conditioning on full blast. "Well, hey, he's the man, right?"

"He practices and keeps his talents up-to-date. When was the last time you tried to use your powers on a girl?"

In middle school, right after he'd changed his name to Eric and learned that didn't reel in the babes. Especially Paula Rizzuto, the foxiest blonde in seventh grade. The last Eric had heard, she'd been divorced twice and was in therapy. More than once, he'd wondered if his bumbling attempts at romance had caused lingering effects. After Paula, Eric had sworn off his powers, preferring to struggle with dating like a stupid mortal. When that hadn't worked, he had caved and sought out Becca's help, her makeover and potions. His last chance and a fairly reasonable alternative.

Insane, he knew. "I appreciate your advice, but I have to do this my way. Can I get that table or not?"

"I already said you could. Bring the girl here. I want to see what you're doing wrong. I'll take notes. Help you out."

This was going to be a fun night.

Becca should have kept her big mouth shut.

Constance, Heather and Zoe accompanied her to her apartment. After all, they were her posse, or to paraphrase what Mere always said to Christina in

Grey's Anatomy—each was Becca's person. In the past, they'd commiserated with her and the others over guys who'd pulverized their dignity. Only Heather had missed out on betrayal, humiliation and a broken heart. She'd never been with a man even in a sweet romantic sense and certainly not physically. That hadn't kept her from joining the rest tonight. None had anything better to do, since they weren't in relationships, and wanted to help Becca get ready for a date she kept insisting was a test run.

"Is that what he called it?" Constance smiled. "And what do you think it is?"

The beginning of endless pain if she didn't keep her cool. All day until now, she'd worked on spells to keep her mind off what might happen tonight. Even though she'd given magic her full respect and attention, her crappy moves had broken two windows, put a virus on her computer and melted the office phone. Heather had had to order a new one.

Becca sprayed mist on her ferns. They filled her bedroom, along with wind chimes, beaded curtains on the windows and Mardi Gras masks on the walls. The decorations were colorful and vibrant. Light-years from her love life. "I think tonight's no big deal for me. For him, it's important, but only because he wants to make certain the potion is working properly before he unleashes his bad boy on the world."

"My, my." Constance tapped her tapered nail against her chin. "Isn't he a cocky little bastard?"

Becca grinned. Eric's glorious shaft had bloomed right before her eyes and jutted brazen and proud. His pendulous balls were equally luscious. "He's hardly little. Hung like a horse is more like it."

"Gave him a blast of your charm, did you?"

Becca wasn't about to disclose what she'd offered him. Weakened by her memories, she leaned against the rocking chair near her brass bed. He was right about men not faking orgasms. They didn't have to. Put any woman between their legs and their cocks jumped to attention, begging for more. "It's unlikely I'll ever have that much allure. However, I think the potion gave him a few extra inches."

"The gift that keeps giving."

They sniggered.

Heather left Becca's walk-in closet, a dress in her right hand, a pants suit in her left. "These are nice."

Constance sniffed. "If she's going to her First Communion." She spoke to Becca. "You don't want to wear white. Sends a man the wrong message."

"I think he knows I'm not a virgin."

"Becca." Color stained Heather's pale cheeks. "No need to talk like that."

Constance pressed her mouth to Becca's ear. "We gotta get that girl laid."

Her shoulders shook with suppressed laughter.

"What about this?" Zoe held up black workout clothes, bought for the gym membership Becca had never used.

"Put that back." Constance pointed at the closet. "She's going on a date, not a funeral at Anytime Fitness."

"It's not a date. It. Is. A. Test. Run." The nth time she'd corrected them. "Tonight could always turn out bad."

Everyone stared at her. Constance's pursed lips warned — don't you dare give me that defeatist shit. Heather's eyes filled with sorrow, her sympathetic nature agreeing with whatever Becca predicted, no matter how bad or humiliating.

Zoe clenched her small fists, ready to rumble. "Say the word and I'll take him out. I'll enjoy it." She trembled with suppressed fury, her anger understandable. The story on how she'd lost her soul to Satan was short and typical. It involved a guy. What else?

"Leave Eric alone, please." Becca prayed Zoe wouldn't hunt him down before the meal in a misguided attempt at protection. "He hasn't done anything." At least, not yet.

She pushed past them, stopped in her closet and shoved one garment after the other aside, rejecting each as being too funky or baggy. A few were laughably innocent, a lot more beyond depraved. She'd worn those outfits to warlock conventions to prove she was ready for any-fucking-thing, which had led to heartbreak.

Tonight, she wanted to keep her wits about her and come off as...

She wasn't certain.

This was nuts. She ran her own business and supported herself better than most women her age, yet she couldn't figure out how to act with a man she liked.

When it came to life, she was hopelessly stupid.

"You're overthinking this, just like everything else," Constance elbowed Becca aside, as she might an irritating child, and studied the outfits.

"What about what you're wearing?" She gestured to Constance's turban and full-length gown both in red-and-white candy cane stripes. "I like it. Want to lend your stuff to me?"

Constance made a dismissive noise. "You wouldn't do it justice. Here."

She pulled out a halter dress. Its flirty skirt landed just below Becca's knees. The wide black belt around the waist sported an ornate gold buckle. Its color matched the soft, shimmering fabric. She'd bought the dress on a whim and never had a chance to wear it.

"This is you." Constance shoved the thing at her. "That's how you should behave tonight—like you." She pointed at the bedroom window. Gauzy sun spilled past the brightly colored beads. Blue, green, yellow and red splashes danced on the walls. "There's not one person out there exactly like Becca Salt. Is there?"

"I would hope not." She chuckled. "One of me in this world is probably enough."

Constance didn't laugh. "Be you, sweetie. If he doesn't like you for the way you look, act, talk, think and everything else about you, even your lousy magic, then he's a fucking idiot."

"Constance." Heather shook her head. "Please, your language." She spoke to Becca. "I do agree, though."

"Me, too." Zoe leaned around the doorjamb, the same as Heather had. "You tell me if he doesn't treat you right. I have your back. Always."

Tears stung Becca's eyes. She couldn't have asked for better friends than these three. She might have been lacking in the looks, figure and guy department but when it came to having a devoted gang, no woman was richer. One day, she hoped they'd find the love they so richly deserved. For her, she wasn't remotely sure but figured she better put on a good show or she'd never get out of here. "He will treat me right. He's a good guy."

"Not since you gave him that potion." Constance smacked Becca's ass. "That man's gonna be two handfuls tonight. Lord, I wish I could be there to see that."

To make certain everything was perfect for this evening, Eric swung by the restaurant to check out the table.

The one Desi set up had red velvet chairs like the others, along with a spotless white tablecloth, fine china and silverware that glinted softly in the room's subdued lighting, a red roses and baby's breath centerpiece and two silver holders complete with red candles, the wicks not lit as yet. Nice, except for what else his uncle had done.

Eric pressed his fingers to his temple and his beginning migraine.

Desi pursed his lips, defensiveness in his eyes. "What?"

"What do you think?" Eric gestured to his and Becca's table as compared to the rest in this room. "Why is this place setting way over here and the others are way over there?"

"You told me you wanted private."

He'd moved the other tables several yards away, leaving this one in emptiness. "This looks like you're quarantining us because we have a disease."

"Love can get rough."

Eric dropped his hand. He and Becca hadn't even slept together yet, at least all the way, which meant them enjoying sex in every possible fashion. That is, if she liked to go the whole nine yards. He prayed she did. He had an unsettling need to be inside her, burrowing as deep as he could, straight to her marrow and soul if possible. Emotions he'd never felt for another woman.

He worried about what she'd put in the last potion.

"Calm down." Desi slapped Eric's back. "You'll live through it."

If he didn't, Desi would have a ringside seat to each painful moment and might flash his homely grin. He was a squat man, his head the size and shape of a bowling ball. Given his huge bald spot, coupled with hair growing in his ears and nostrils, he looked like the 'after' picture for Becca's first potion. Thankfully, his palms were smooth. "Don't even think about using your powers on her."

He tensed his doughy shoulders the way he always did when he wanted to argue a point to infinity. "Why not? You won't use yours. What's the matter with you? Don't you never wanna settle down?"

"Not with someone I have to shoot through the heart with a magical arrow to make her mine then repeat the process periodically, like a booster shot, so she doesn't stray to other guys. If any woman keeps me around for the long haul, I want it to be because of who I really am, warts and all, not anything else."

"No wonder you're single. Them warts you mentioned aren't a selling point to the ladies, you know?"

"No one's perfect. She can take me as I am or not at all." Big talk, especially when it came to Becca. Eric sensed he'd do backflips over broken glass if it made her smile, and like him.

Desi lifted his face to the beveled ceiling. Frescos showed chubby winged babies, a mortal's version of Cupid. "You young people."

"Yeah, we're the worst. Come on, I'll help you put these tables back the way they should be, then I have to go home and get ready."

"Now? You got hours to prepare. You don't even have to shave." Desi pushed to his toes, which made him about five-five, and squinted. "You do finally shave, don't you?"

Eric arched one eyebrow. "Since I hit puberty nearly two decades ago."

"Hey, don't blame me if your beard isn't what you want it to be."

Since when hadn't it been? Eric rubbed his cheeks and chin then slumped in relief. His stubble was bristly, as it should be at this hour. Becca's potion hadn't changed that. The bulge between his legs was the same size it had been earlier in the day when she'd commented on it.

He adored how she teased. Her banter made him feel important and special.

"Hey." Desi backhanded Eric's belly. "Quit admiring your stuff. There are ladies present."

Eric waved to his aunt and cousins. They huddled together at the maître d's station. "They don't know anything about my date tonight, do they?"

The girls slapped their hands over their mouths to stifle their giggles. His aunt looked at Eric indulgently, her way of giving him a high-five.

"Not at all." Desi smirked, not trying to hide the fact that he lied. "Let's move these tables."

As a rule, Eric didn't primp. He always shaved, brushed his teeth, showered and threw on his clothes. Stretchy boxers from now on, a fresh shirt, pants or khakis, socks and shoes. Being clean and neat summed up his love affair with his appearance.

Tonight, he couldn't decide what the fuck to wear. He held up his shirts in various browns, blues, beiges or whites and stared at himself in the mirror. Trying to see what Becca would.

A stud or a dud.

He wondered if the potion had caused his indecision, unless it had made him vain. One of the few problems he'd never had before and didn't want now.

He decided to wear his beige shirt and brown pants.

He pulled them off the hangers then slipped them right back on and regarded his blue shirt, then the white, then the —

For shit's sake, make up your mind. You're not a girl. In record speed, he forced himself to dress and checked the time. If all went well and Becca showed up, he'd see her in forty-five minutes.

That is, unless he arrived late. That's what studs did. They kept a woman waiting, guessing and hoping. The ladies seemed to love that.

He hadn't a clue if Becca would. Or if his thoughtless delay would piss her off and make her leave.

Eric sank to his bed, reduced to indecision like a pimply teen. All he had to do now was worry whether Becca would kiss him goodnight or not and he'd be twelve again.

Or the same as he'd been before the potion.

He arrived thirty minutes early and stayed in his car, staring at Desiderio's spumoni-colored façade, figuring he looked as sick as its pale green shutters. The potion wasn't working any longer. Eric knew it for certain now. He physically ached to see Becca, his shoulders and neck burning, his unmanageable desire mounting by the second. He wanted to please her so much it frightened him. With other women, he'd been interested and eager, though not to this degree.

This had to stop before he made a fool of himself and screwed up the night. He pulled out his smartphone ready to call Becca's office and beg Heather, or even Zoe, to make a run to this parking lot with a jug of the potion. It sure as hell had made him behave like a beast in the treatment room.

When he'd told Becca to undress, it was as though someone else was talking, a person he didn't know but liked. He'd had no problem ordering her around and expecting her to obey, not even considering that she might kick him in the balls and tell him to leave.

She hadn't. Becca had treated his cock and nuts as something precious that she had to have.

Eric wanted to be that demanding again.

He drummed his fingers on the steering wheel and considered whether there would be enough time to have someone mix the potion, bring it down here then pay her off to keep her mouth shut so Becca wouldn't know about it.

Being so shy and apologetic, Heather might not be cool with lying. Zoe probably would, given she was a mean little thing. However, she might also put arsenic or cyanide in his potion.

He debated the pros and cons so long twenty minutes passed before he noticed. Damn, it was too late for magic now. He'd have to pretend to be a bad boy. If he were lucky, Becca wouldn't notice the difference between the way he'd acted in the treatment room and how he'd behave tonight.

A hearse pulled up to Desiderio's front door.

No one could have died. If they had, an ambulance would have pulled up first to take the body to a funeral home. Maybe the driver was here for takeout.

Eric leaned against his steering wheel for a closer look.

Zoe sat in the driver's seat.

An urge to flee hit him hard and fast.

Before he could move, the passenger door popped open and Becca stepped out.

His legs went weak.

The muggy breeze ruffled her hair. The lights in the parking lot skimmed its reddish color and deepened the passionate tint, making it beyond provocative.

Eric opened his door.

Liquid gold couldn't have fit her better than the dress she wore. The top molded itself to her sumptuous breasts. The skirt clung to her hips and thighs. The gentle wind lifted the hem.

She held her skirt down with both hands as Marilyn Monroe had done with hers in the famous still from *The Seven Year Itch*.

Becca said something to Zoe, eased her purse strap over her arm and closed the door. Zoe floored her death-mobile, burning rubber on her way out.

Eric suspected she wasn't pleased with tonight's events.

Aroused and possessed by something he didn't understand, he rushed through the lot and caught up with Becca as she reached the stairs leading to the front door.

He slipped his arm around her waist.

She looked at his hold on her and lifted her face to his. Gone was the dramatic makeup, leaving only Becca. Softness, heat and desire flared in her beautiful eyes. Surrender, too.

She touched his cheek.

An invitation Eric couldn't resist. Easing her into him, he fitted his mouth to hers.

Chapter Seven

Becca sagged against Eric, lost in his deep, lingering kiss and loving caress. Any resistance she might have owned in order to protect her dignity and heart was a distant memory. He tasted better than she recalled. His desire celebrated her most romantic and wanton fantasies.

Countless times, she'd dreamed of a moment like this. A guy, her guy, greeting her with unrestrained passion, stark lust and aching tenderness. The best emotion that existed. Proof lay in how carefully he held her and the gentle pressure from his lips. His hunger barely controlled.

She prayed he'd let loose. To give him a nudge, she melted into him, a willing prisoner of his masculine power.

He groaned ruggedly, dipped his tongue into her mouth and explored with reverence and need that said he wanted her. She mattered.

For now.

Was it enough?

To a woman starved for a simple caress and validation that she was attractive and worthy, this was the greatest high possible. More dangerous than the most potent and addictive drug.

Too bad it wasn't real. Tonight wasn't even a date. It would end.

Intellectually, she knew the truth. Her battered heart said "Fuck it. Don't deny me this or him." Becca wreathed her arm over Eric's shoulder and pressed her fingertips into his muscular back. She returned his kiss without guile or artifice, protection removed, leaving her more naked and vulnerable than she'd been in the treatment room.

They strained to get closer, each trying to achieve greater intimacy. The sounds he made were uninhibited and enchanting.

Applause broke out.

The clapping didn't interrupt Eric's craving.

Becca's, either.

Wolf whistles pierced the relative quiet and hurt her ears.

She pulled her mouth from his.

Three young couples stood behind them, waiting to get past to the restaurant stairway. The women beamed. The guys whistled and grinned. They took Becca in briefly then nodded and winked at Eric. The universal male signal that said they approved how he'd scored.

Becca blushed, which was silly. She wasn't embarrassed. So much happiness engulfed her, she wanted to squeal her delight.

Smiling, Eric eased her from the stairs and gestured the group toward the entrance.

A brunette sexy enough to be a Dallas Cowboys cheerleader or a server in a Hooters restaurant stopped at Eric's side. "Bad boy," she purred. "You behave now."

She drew her tongue over her ruby lips.

Becca wanted to bite her.

Eric tightened his arm around her waist and spoke to Ms. Nympho. "Not a chance." He snuggled his cheek against Becca's.

Stunned at his public possessiveness, she rested her palm on his chest and claimed him, too.

The girl offered a patronizing smile — the way cool kids in school behaved to the lesser mortals among them. Given her face and bod, she wasn't a stranger to her physical gifts. She grabbed her date's hand and led him up the stairs as she might a trained seal even though he was prettier than she was.

For once, Becca didn't envy people like that.

Eric rested his forehead against her temple. "Hi."

His breath warmed her better than the sun ever had. He smelled so clean and masculine, she longed to rub against him and mark him with her scent. Like a cat.

She was losing it, and they'd only been together for a few minutes. No telling what an hour or more would lead to. Not that she would consider anything that awesome and scary. She'd promised herself this wouldn't be more than a test run. Preparing him for other women. Beautiful and built babes.

He rubbed his nose against her cheek.

She forgot how to breathe. "Hey."

"Did I say how amazing you look?"

If he had, Becca didn't recall. She'd been too focused on sucking his tongue and drowning in his warmth. "I don't see how you could have noticed. Your eyes have been closed." She mimicked the brunette's purr. "Bad boy."

He chuckled. "Let's see if we can change that." He held her hands out and took her in from top to bottom and back. An exceedingly slow journey.

His scrutiny rattled her and made her stomach churn. It took enormous will to act confident at what he'd think and say. Too many times, others had disparaged her looks. To harden herself against everyone's judgment, Becca had taken to dressing unconventionally and told herself she no longer cared what the rest of the world thought.

Eric's approval was important to her. She wasn't ashamed for feeling that way. It was honest. Who she was. What Constance had advised her to be.

"Wow." His eyes glazed over. "You're gorgeous."

Becca would have laughed but didn't want to ruin the moment. "Thanks. You look great, too." His physical gifts beat hers by a mile. He was right out of *GQ*, casual yet elegant in his beige sports coat, espresso-colored pants and cream shirt.

She turned her wrists, wanting to be free so she could touch him.

He held on to her briefly before letting go.

His delay surprised her. If this had been a normal date, she would have hoped he was trying to prove his attraction. Since tonight was a test run, she figured he could be showing off his newly released beast.

Before she could figure it out, he smiled. The joy reached his eyes and stroked her soul.

She craved another kiss. Knowing how unwise that would be, she settled on straightening his brown-and-tan striped tie then thumbed her lipstick from his mouth.

He licked her finger.

If it hadn't been uncool or maybe weird, she would have tasted the faint moisture he'd left on her. She should have offered her hand so he could lead her into the restaurant like a lovesick pet, but moving wasn't something she could do.

He didn't sprint up the steps either.

They stared at each other while the world rolled by. Tires whooshed over asphalt. A horn honked. Laughter rang in the distance, the hearty sounds decidedly male.

A door opened and a classical Italian opera joined the other noise. The female singer wailed her guts out followed by loud throat clearing.

Becca looked over.

A chunky man with a wide face and balding head leaned out of the restaurant. "So, there you are, Er—ah..." He hunched his shoulders and talked through his teeth. "There you are, Er-ic. Thought you weren't coming. You're late."

This was news and not the most welcomed kind. She spoke softly to Eric. "Is he joining us?"

"Not at our table. He owns this place. That's Uncle Desi," Eric whispered. "Unfortunately, my real uncle."

Her delight returned at them having dinner alone, even though the arrangements shouldn't have mattered to her. "You poor guy." She kept her voice low as he had. "I see the resemblance."

Eric smacked her butt.

Becca grinned at his playfulness, which she'd rarely experienced with other men. Luckily, Desi couldn't see Eric's flirtatious swat. "Better be careful what you do. I sense he doesn't like you very much."

"He doesn't like that I changed my name and refuse to come near a stupid arrow."

"What?"

Ignoring Becca's question, Eric escorted her up the stairs. "Uncle Desi. Sorry for being late. I hope the kitchen staff and servers didn't mind too much. If they do, I'll apologize to each. Our table's ready, right?"

"Talk smart all you want, it's not gonna change nothing." He blocked the door.

Eric's arm tightened around her waist. "Look, I was kidding, okay? Can we go in? Please?"

"Don't I get to meet your date?"

"Desi—where'd you go?" the older female voice called from inside the restaurant. "We need you."

He spoke to Becca and Eric. "I'll be back. Don't you two move from that spot. I mean it." He closed the door.

She bumped Eric's shoulder. "He seems nice, but kind of disturbed."

"That's just his personality. He's obnoxious, but no danger to himself or others."

Becca struggled not to laugh. "I meant, he seems upset about me being here. You didn't tell him I'm part-witch, did you? Maybe you should assure him this is a test run for the real thing. It might calm him down."

Eric stared at her. Indignation crossed his face.

She couldn't imagine why. "What?"

He shoved his hands in his pockets and leaned against the wrought-iron railing. As far from her as he could get, unless he bounded down the stairs. "He doesn't know you're part-witch. He enjoys humiliating me. He'll probably haul out my baby pictures before our meal is over. I shouldn't have brought you here, but you chose Italian, and since this is the best place for..."

Becca stopped listening. She tried to imagine Eric as an infant. Naked yet innocent.

"I knew it would have been better if you'd chosen French or Cajun." He blew out a sigh.

She smiled. "I'd like to see your baby pictures."

His face went redder than her hair. "I don't think so."

"I bet you were adorable."

He made a nasty face that said she was a cretin. Totally out of character for someone who was too nice. Or had been, before drinking those potions.

Becca stroked his tie. "How are you feeling?"

"Feeling?"

"Yeah. What's going on inside you?"

His face went slack, the way it might if she'd accused him of premature ejaculation. "Nothing."

"Come on." She needed to know if the potion was helping or hurting. As far as she was concerned, he turned her inside out. He was tender and commanding, funny and hotter than hell. She wanted him more with each passing second even though she knew how dangerous that was to her heart. The other women out there hadn't a clue what they were in for once Eric entered their lives. "Tell me."

"You don't want to know."

"Sure, I do."

"Fine. I feel like this." He cupped her head.

She thrummed with desire and expected him to kiss her.

He drew her closer and took in her features, lingering on her mouth. His lips parted in what might have been unbridled lust and wonder. Crazy, she knew. His behavior had to be from the potion. She should have been disappointed. Excitement and anticipation kept her from it.

Eric ran his thumb over her skull.

Delight rippled down her spine to her pussy. She was already wet and getting damper by the second. Her pulse pounded against her throat. She tried to swallow, but couldn't.

"And I feel like this." He tilted his head and lowered his mouth to hers in a kiss unlike the few others they'd shared. This one was slow, deep and achingly sensuous. Skilled beyond belief and holding immeasurable hope and promise.

Her knees gave out.

She slipped her arms around his neck and pushed his tongue aside with hers, hungering for what these few minutes would bring — his bold desire for her fueled by his new personality and the potion. That wasn't what she needed for the long run, but Becca couldn't bring herself to care about reality during kickass moments like these. She'd had so little of this in her life.

"Eros, please." Uncle Desi tapped his foot. "Control yourself."

Becca ignored the old guy.

Eric tugged Becca closer and held her tighter against his massive erection.

No matter how many years passed, she'd always remember this.

Desi muttered something that didn't sound good.

Not wanting to cause a serious family rift, she freed her mouth from Eric's and rested her forehead against his. Pulling in adequate air wasn't an option.

He planted his hands on her shoulders and turned her around. "Uncle Desi, this is Becca Salt. Becca, this is my Uncle Desi."

He sandwiched her hand between his and squeezed gently. "Nice to meet you. I want to apologize for Eros — Eric." He mumbled something beneath his breath then threw Eric a look that said his nephew was acting like a pig. Facing her, Desi softened his bluster. "He's usually so polite. I don't know what's gotten into him."

Becca did and it killed the wonder she'd experienced scant moments before. Whatever happened between her and Eric tonight, it wasn't real. She had to remember that. "It's all right. This is just—"

"Our first date." Eric held her against him.

She guessed he didn't want his uncle knowing they weren't a couple.

Desi's frown said Eric was nuts. "You think things between you two are gonna cool down from here?" He inclined his bulky head toward Becca. "Look at her." He offered a sweet smile and kissed her fingertips. "You're exquisite."

Becca was beginning to understand where Eric had gotten his charm.

"Come on." Desi folded her arm over his and pulled her from Eric. "Let me show you to your table."

She looked over.

Eric stared at her gold heels, her calves, thighs and ass, as if they were also on the menu tonight.

So maybe the potion hadn't worn off, as Eric had feared. Could be it had a time-release mechanism similar to Contac cold capsules.

He had no other way to explain his disregard for propriety, around his straitlaced uncle, no less. Never had Eric gone at the other women he'd brought here as he had at Becca, with a lot more to come. He hoped. Like a faithful dog, he followed her to their table, delighting in how her dress slid over her legs. The shimmery fabric resembled water reflecting countless golden flames.

Her back was smooth and flawless. She had an exceptionally kissable spine. Since time had begun, guys had enjoyed wet dreams about an ass as sweet as hers. Waking up from that vision was the worst torture possible.

Every time she glanced over, he had to stiffen his legs or risk sinking to the floor.

She smiled tentatively, but softly too.

Another look like that and Eric didn't know what he'd do except take her right there, right then, in front of Desi, his aunt, the restaurant patrons and Jupiter, too, if he watched from his castle in the sky.

Putting his lust to good use, Eric beat Desi to Becca's chair and offered his hand.

She curled her fingers around his.

Every hair he owned stood on end. He felt a thousand feet tall and more powerful than Superman yet weakened too. Once she sat, he kissed her knuckles like a knight or Cupid's descendant would.

She stared at her hand.

Panic hit him. He prayed she wouldn't laugh at his dumb move no bad boy would have made.

Pink blossomed in her cheeks. She glanced at him shyly, but pleasure showed on her face.

Thrilled, he sank into his chair and spread his legs wide, giving his balls and cock a chance to relax and breathe.

Desi rocked on his heels and regarded them intently.

Eric went from harder-than-steel to flaccid in a second. "Thanks for the table." He prayed his uncle wouldn't say anything embarrassing or bad. "You can send our server over whenever you want."

"I'm your server tonight, so you behave. As for you…" Desi winked at Becca. "I'm bringing you our finest house wine and tonight's special. *Delizioso.*" With an Italian chef's flair, he kissed his fingertips and bent from the waist. "That is, if you don't mind."

She smiled.

Looked a little unnatural to Eric, the way it would if her thong had dug into the wrong places. She had to be wearing one. There hadn't been any panty lines beneath her skirt.

"I don't mind at all." She spoke warmly to Desi. "That's very sweet of you. Thanks."

Desi slapped Eric's shoulder. "She's a gem." To her, he practically cooed, "Be right back, *bella signora.*"

He hurried away.

Confusion sped across Becca's lovely features.

Eric figured he'd better explain. "He never acts like this. Not once has he called my aunt beautiful lady, at least in my presence."

Her eyes widened slightly. "Is that what he said to me? He is nice."

"No, he's not. He's a mean prick at times, but honest to a fault. You are beautiful."

A deeper flush than before stained her chest, throat and face.

If Eric had to guess, he would have said she was torn between laughing and crying at his comment. He had no idea why.

She laid her dainty purse on the table. "I hate to bring this up…"

Whenever a woman began a conversation like that, it couldn't be good. He kept his peace, hoping his silence would derail anything bad.

She fidgeted.

He was too afraid to move. This reminded him of their first conversation in her office when she had wanted his memories removed. She couldn't have circled back to that. A pain twisted in his belly. He couldn't stand the suspense. "What?"

"You don't want Desi to know about you taking the potion, do you?"

Her bringing that up was as bad as the memory thing, both about business rather than them getting to know each other and liking what they learned. Surely, she didn't behave with her other dates as she did with him. Hot one minute, tepid the next then coolly professional. He hoped her next step wouldn't be to freeze him out entirely. "None of his business. I'm fully grown."

Becca stared at his belt and leaned up.

He supposed to see the prize behind his fly that the table hid. A good sign.

She sagged in her chair. "How are you feeling?"

Horny as hell. Frustrated as shit. Wanting what? Everything? Maybe. Eric didn't know. He didn't want to think. Hell, feeling was using his energy. "I thought I already answered that outside when we kissed."

Her lips were slightly bruised and swollen from his passion. Her expression blurred and her gaze turned inward.

Food was the last thing he wanted now. They had to get out of here to someplace private.

She blinked and regained her composure. "I meant, are there any unexpected effects?"

That's not what she'd meant at all. "Nothing I wasn't able to handle."

"Like what?" Distrust filled her eyes. "Tell me."

He wasn't certain what she expected him to say. That he'd screwed every woman at his condominium complex and in the restaurant parking lot before he'd attacked her? "No reason to worry. I merely shaved my palms and tongue before I came here."

She stared at his hands and mouth.

"I was kidding. At least about my palms." He made a gagging sound as he had in the treatment room before he spit up hair.

Becca rubbed her temple but did giggle.

He loved the sound. The same went for her delighted moans during their kiss. No music could match its power. Certainly, not the crap Desi played in this place. One more piercing shriek from the singer and Eric figured his teeth would crack. "I also had to get new underwear."

Becca gave him a sideways look. "You're into stretchy boxers finally."

"Have to be." He leaned against the table and kept his voice low. "I need the support. I have a lot to carry around."

A throaty laugh poured from her. Embarrassment flashed across her face. She glanced at the other patrons to see if they'd noticed. They hadn't. She regarded their tables and frowned. "Why are we sitting so far away from everyone?"

"So, Desi can torture us."

"You're just sensitive. He's a real sweetheart. Reminds me of my dad."

"Oh, yeah?" Eric liked how the candlelight brought out the fire in her hair and turned her pale skin to ivory. "Tell me about him and your mom."

Becca waved away his request. "Nothing to tell."

"You don't want me to know? Or you don't think I meant what I just said, because tonight isn't real, we're simply playing at this."

Hurt and uncertainty pinched her features.

Eric wanted to cut out his tongue for making her uncomfortable. Afraid he'd say something even worse, he clammed up.

She shrugged. "Yeah, I guess that's it. I don't want to bore you."

That wasn't possible. She was Becca Salt. A witch who couldn't concoct a useable potion to save her life, owned a weirdo business, had friends straight from the depths of Hell, looked amazing in everything she wore, had features that could only be considered stunning and a heart Eric wanted to touch. Why, he still didn't know and wasn't going to question his feelings. "You won't bore me, I promise. The only time I nod off is after sex. But only for a few minutes."

He didn't want to give her the wrong impression.

Becca nodded seriously. "You're the man. However, despite your stamina, we probably shouldn't go at it on our table or under it, huh?"

"Probably not. That's what treatment rooms and condos were made for."

She got that dreamy look again, perhaps because she pictured him naked and harder than stone. "Sex does make paying the mortgage much easier."

"I'm not complaining."

"You better not." Desi cradled a bottle of his finest wine with the same tenderness most men reserve for their first-born sons. "Complaining about what?"

Becca smiled softly. "Being thirsty."

Desi's ruddy face darkened further at her feminine charm. "Of course. I kept you waiting too long. Forgive me." He filled her glass and ignored Eric's.

She gestured to it. "I think he'd like some, too."

"No more than half a glass." Desi poured less than that. "You're driving. Both hands on the wheel, eyes on the road not on her no matter how much you can't help yourself."

"Desi." Eric's aunt tapped his shoulder. "You're needed." She gave Becca and Eric an indulgent smile then glared at her husband.

He muttered something beneath his breath and spoke to them. "Be right back."

Eric waited until Desi was far enough away to avoid overhearing. "So, your dad's like that? You poor thing."

"You have no idea. If I use a word stronger than darn, he lectures me on how a proper lady should behave."

Eric tapped his glass to hers in a toast. "And how's that?"

"Damned if I know. I keep getting it wrong."

They laughed.

He recalled their moments in the treatment room and outside this place. Both epic. "Like I said, I'm not complaining. You can tell your dad for me that you're perfect just as you are."

Becca lowered her glass without tasting the wine and averted her gaze, her mood back to uncertain.

He pretended not to notice her reaction to what he'd said. An honest compliment from a man shouldn't have surprised her, but she'd had a shitty adolescence as he'd had. To ease the strained silence between them, he sipped his wine, savoring its rich body and fruity flavor. At three thousand bucks a bottle, it more than matched its price, but didn't come close to tasting as wonderful as she had.

Nature had created Becca's mouth for a hungry man and made her curves perfect to sate lust and to offer comfort afterward. How any male could have found her wanting was beyond Eric. The fools she'd grown up with must have been blind. "You had a tough time in school, just like I did."

He hoped their common bond would relax her.

Becca lifted her eyebrows. "That's putting it mildly."

"Tell me."

She gestured dismissively then gave him a questioning look. "You're sure? It's really ancient history."

"Are you certain about that?" Her skin was smooth and flawless, not even a mole. No wrinkles, either. "How old are you exactly?"

Becca choked on her wine, coughed and put out her hand. "I'm okay." Her voice rasped. "Twenty-seven. You?"

"Thirty-two. In mortal years?"

"Me or you?"

Smiling, he pointed at her.

"You do know that asking a woman her age or her weight makes you a jerk."

"I'm many things, but definitely not a jerk. I think your weight is fine. I've already told you, most women are too skinny."

She got that faraway look again. One filled with gratitude and sin he enjoyed. "Ah, mortal. That is, I'm twenty-seven in human years."

"Is that why you attended a regular school growing up?"

Becca fingered her glass. "Dad insisted upon it. Like I said, he's mortal. Assured me it'd be a great experience."

"Well yeah, if you're a cheerleader or football captain."

She nodded knowingly.

"As I already revealed, my parents insisted the same with me. We both know how that turned out." Eric threw back his head and opened his mouth as if someone had punched him out.

She laughed.

He grinned, proud he'd got a positive reaction from her. "Did you pretend things were okay at school? That you enjoyed it?"

"What other choice was there? I didn't want to hurt him with the truth. I'd do anything to please my dad."

"Just like your mom always has?"

"Oh, yeah." She glowed. "They're so much in love it's nauseating."

"How did they end up together, given they're so different? Does he even know she's a witch?"

Becca laughed so hard her face turned red. "Ah, yeah. He's aware. They met after her date with a warlock tanked. He'd been flirting all night with other witches and my mom had enough. Good for her. In my book, she should have castrated him. Instead, she did the adult thing and told him that he either gave her his full attention when they were together or they were through. He laughed. After he used his powers to strip her bare, both her clothes and power, he left her on a deserted road. He said when she apologized to him for being such a bitch, he'd be back. She refused and walked in the cold, rainy night alone. At the time, my dad was a truck driver. He owns his own company now. She flagged him down. He picked her up and the rest, as they say, is history."

Romeo and Juliet it wasn't, mainly because her parents had a happy ending, the only thing that counted. "He wasn't surprised or appalled by her powers? I'm assuming they returned fully."

"Within twenty-four hours. I can't say he was thrilled, but only because of the possible fallout. You know, exorcisms, the feds wanting to experiment on her to see what makes a witch tick, stuff like that. However, he accepted her for who she is, the same as she does with him."

Sounded like the perfect romance, certainly better than Bella and Edward in *Twilight*, a truly dumb film.

Desi stalked to them and growled. "Bread and olive oil." He put the basket and bottles on the table. "Enjoy."

Eric couldn't help but tease. "You're sure you want that?"

"My wife says you should, so you should." Desi clenched his jaw. "Okay?"

"Send her my everlasting gratitude."

Desi spoke to Becca. "He gives you trouble, you let me know. I'll take care of him."

"Don't worry. She has Zoe to do that." Eric wiggled his eyebrows at her. "Right?"

Becca lowered her face to hide her smile.

"Zoe?" Desi lifted his shoulders. "Who's that?"

"Becca's pit bull." Eric didn't want to say what Zoe really was, or at least what he thought she might be, and worry Desi. "Little thing but mean."

Becca's shoulders shook with her laughter, "Careful. She has unusually good hearing."

Desi frowned. "What are you two talking about?"

Eric's aunt tapped his shoulder.

"Oh, hell." He spoke to her. "I'm not bothering them."

"Then come and help us, like you're supposed to."

Grumbling, he left.

Becca gave Eric a scolding look. "Pit bull?"

"I didn't want to worry him. He never would have left the table if I said she was a demon. She is, right? I mean, with the sulfur smell, flames in her eyes, smoking hair and all." He shuddered. "She couldn't possibly think that's attractive to men."

"It is to other demons. However, Zoe's doing her best to convert back to the mortal way of doing things, like when she was human."

Eric recalled when Becca needed her phone and Zoe had resisted using her dark powers to get the thing. He poured the oil and broke his bread apart. "That still coming along okay?"

"She hasn't possessed or pulverized anyone for months and has no plan to do so. However, she might make an exception for you."

He'd already figured as much but smiled at Becca's teasing. With the bread lightly soaked in oil, he offered it to her. "Taste…enjoy."

To his delight, she scooted her chair closer and allowed him to slip the bite into her mouth. Oil slid over her bottom lip. Eric captured it with his finger and licked it off.

Becca's chewing slowed and stopped. "This is really good."

He sensed she wasn't talking about the bread, but the bewitching time they were having.

"It gets even better." A promise he intended to keep by feeding her. The bread was soon forgotten. He nibbled on her fingertips. She licked his thumb.

Once Desi delivered their appetizer and made himself scarce, Becca delighted Eric by slipping Camembert cheese and a marinated artichoke heart between his lips.

He licked the spiced marinade from her palm.

She blushed and smiled.

He just about died from the happiest feeling he could remember.

They fed each other the *pasta e fagioli* and laughed about the horrible pasta artwork they'd created for their parents as kids.

"I did one of my dad's trucks." Becca accepted the cheese Eric offered her, chewed and swallowed. "He gushed like mad. Said it was the best drawing of a piggybank he'd ever seen. I wouldn't speak to him for days."

Eric grinned. "That'll teach him. I did Cupid on steroids. Arrows flying everywhere, taking the bad fuckers down like Vin Diesel always does. My mother cried and suggested therapy. Dad said no son of his was going to a shrink. He signed me up for ballroom dancing. Said that'd straighten me out."

Becca bent over from laughter. "You poor baby." She heaved in a breath. "Sorry. I'm not laughing at you."

He already knew that. His heart opened even more to her. "It's okay. After so many years, I find it kind of funny, too."

She snickered. "What did you learn?"

"Not to do artwork any longer."

Her head fell back with her newest laughter. "No, I mean dance-wise."

Not a lot, but for her he'd learn the latest moves so they could take in some nightclubs during their next times out. "Let's just say I can hold my own with anyone over eighty."

"Stop." Her shoulders trembled. "I can't take much more."

Eric could have done this forever. No other woman had laughed so much with him.

They enjoyed their medium-rare steaks next, the meat seared and seasoned to perfection. He pretended to accept the slice Becca offered him but lightly nipped her thumb instead. She giggled. He slipped steak between her lips. She tongued the juices and sucked his finger.

Captivated, he kissed her wrist.

She pressed her mouth to his palm.

Only sex would have been more mind-boggling, but not as tender.

While they molested non-intimate body parts on each other, Desi returned. "You two are still hungry, I can tell." He gave them his sternest look.

Reluctantly, they broke apart.

"You have to try my tiramisu. You especially." Desi pointed at Becca. "I promise it will be the best you've ever tasted. Decadently layered with mascarpone cheese and cocoa and brimming with espresso." He spoke to Eric. "The coffee's so you don't fall asleep while you're driving because you had too much wine."

He hadn't finished the little Desi had given him. Nor had Becca polished off hers. They'd forgotten the booze, not needing it, clicking during their meal like a couple who'd been married for years.

They stared at each other now as new lovers were inclined to do.

Desi handed Becca a fork. "When I bring the dessert, you can share it with my nephew." He frowned at Eric. "If that's okay with you."

It wasn't. He'd never been as aroused. Becca's tight nipples pressed against her stretchy dress, calling to the beast within him. "Actually, I'm more than full. Clear to bursting. Becca?"

Her color was high, eyes hooded, her attention meant solely for him. "Me, too. Couldn't eat another bite."

That's what he wanted to hear.

Desi didn't budge. "I'll wrap it up. You can take it with you."

Eric didn't want to wait that long. He was past the point of no return and figured Becca was too. She ran her foot up his leg. "Another time. You have my AmEx number." He helped her from her chair.

Desi scowled. "You're leaving already?"

To Eric, it seemed they'd been here his entire life, yet not long at all.

"We have plans." She elbowed Eric. "Don't we."

He hoped her program for what remained of tonight was as good as the one he envisioned. "Yeah. A show. Movie. Starts in a few minutes. Isn't that right?"

She nodded and offered her hand to Desi. "Thanks. Everything was great."

He hugged her. "Come back then. Soon."

That wouldn't happen until Eric sated himself with her. He hadn't a clue how long that might take. The way he felt now, it could be weeks or months.

He escorted Becca through the packed dining room to the outside. The air had cooled somewhat, a pleasant caress compared to the earlier suffocating heat. Not that it tempered what was going on inside him. Fevered and wanting, he hurried Becca down the stairs and took her in his arms.

They kissed as they would have if Desi had spiked their food with turbo-charged aphrodisiacs, which was idiotic. Eric knew real when he felt it, and this couldn't have been more genuine. Never had he wanted a woman as much as he did her. He suspected she felt the same about him. Becca definitely didn't hold back. She sucked his lower lip, thrust her tongue into his mouth and ground her pussy into his cock.

Magic couldn't compete with this.

She broke free and wheezed in air. "Where'd you park?"

He pointed. With his arm around her waist, he hurried her to his Mercedes.

Becca held back. "No."

She couldn't have changed her mind already. He hadn't done or said anything to make her do so. "No? Why is that?"

"Your car's too far away." She glanced at the others in the lot.

"We can't break in and use a stranger's." Eric was horny, not nuts. He wanted to wrestle with her, not the police. "We'd be arrested."

"Right. What's over there?" She pointed.

"The restaurant's al fresco dining area. Closed for an upgrade. You want to go there?"

"Think your uncle will come out?"

It was doubtful. Even if Desi did, Eric didn't care. He figured the amazing potion from Becca's mom had given him brass balls. Taking command, as he should, he led Becca around the building. The tiny white lights were off, the wrought-iron tables and chairs empty. Shadows provided privacy though not total darkness.

Her eyes sparkled from the faint illumination bleeding past the building. Desire and submission to what they both wanted shone on her face.

He gathered Becca in his arms, amazed at how soft and lush she was. All woman. Nearly more than he could bear. He pressed his mouth to her ear. "Are you wearing a thong?"

"No."

Disappointed, he forged ahead. "Panties?"

"No."

That didn't make sense. "A girdle?"

"What? No." She elbowed him.

He put on a show and groaned. If she wasn't wearing a thong, panties or a girdle, that only left… "Nothing?"

"Bingo."

If his cock could have sung, it would have. She was full of surprises tonight. Her no-underwear state alone should have had him dancing about what she wanted. However, he still tried to read her mood so he knew precisely what she felt. When it came to women, he'd never been sure. With her, the problem was magnified by his desire to thrill and please her. He should have asked what she expected, but didn't want to break the spell they'd woven around each other. "Thanks."

She eased back and looked at him. "For not wearing underwear?"

"For not telling me until now." He cupped her ass, naked except for her thin dress. Her warmth poured into him. His brain turned to mush. "If you'd done so in the restaurant, I might have stabbed Desi to get him to back off so we could get out here."

Her head lolled to the side. "You really would have done that?"

"Naw." He pressed his face to her neck and drowned in her scent. "A threat would have worked better than violence and would have avoided an arrest and being grilled. I'd much rather be with you than the cops."

"I see." She kissed him breathless. While he struggled to fill his lungs, she placed her purse on the nearest table and pulled out a chair. With one high-heel sandal propped on the seat, she eased her skirt up her leg. "So, what are you waiting for?"

Chapter Eight

The muggy breeze ruffled Becca's dress, as she hoped. The fabric rippled against her calf and thigh, inviting Eric to explore her nudity.

He stared at her leg.

If she hadn't known better, she would have suspected he'd never seen a woman's naked limb before.

The ridge in his throat bobbed with his hard swallow. His gaze devoured her. He scanned their surroundings and took off his jacket. Lightly, he whapped the garment against the table behind her.

The mosaic-tiled top pinged.

She spoke quietly. "Are we going to lie down on that?"

"Not both of us. Hang tight."

Easier said than done. If her nipples got any harder, they'd poke holes in her top. Her pussy was so freaking damp no matter how much the breeze licked those folds, they'd never dry out. She wanted this more than air, food, water or all the riches the universe owned. The only thing that could have increased her craving was a future filled with him and these pleasures. Not expecting that, she couldn't wait much longer for this. "Want me to help?"

"Nope. I'm finished." Eric spread his jacket over the dusted tiles and offered his hand.

Becca caressed his fingers as she would something priceless, because that's what he was—a god among gods.

Naked need flared in his eyes. He embraced her readily and possessively, in a way he hadn't before.

Her excitement sparked to an alarming level, leaving her lightheaded. They were really going to climb all over each other out here. In public.

Somehow, it seemed reasonable.

He kissed her hard and unyieldingly with a right she'd not only given him, but one he'd taken as the newest member of the Bad Boys Club.

Probably not a good thing, but not a matter she could resist.

He stroked her back, cupped her ass and pulled her close so her cunt could know the wonders his cock would soon deliver.

Reinforced concrete had nothing on his shaft. Becca's heart sputtered and raced.

Eric savored her lips with far more gusto than he had their meal. He angled his head to the left and right to sink his tongue even deeper into her mouth.

A gift she accepted without hesitation. She tasted him greedily and gripped his shirt to keep him as close as possible. Their parting would come soon enough. She didn't want to think about that and lost herself in their kiss.

He ground his hips into hers. His rigid shaft pressed against her cleft, wanting in.

Becca craved the same. Waiting another second was too cruel. She tore her mouth free.

His breaths rasped. "What's wrong?"

"Nothing. I'm ready."

"Fuck, I passed that hours ago. On the table. Lie back. Now."

Even in the treatment room, he hadn't sounded as husky or insistent, and he'd been out of control then.

This was totally bad. Becca leaned into him.

"Doing okay?" He rubbed her back.

His strokes were a miracle—light yet strong, tender but hungry. She trembled. "Yeah. Just a little dizzy. Give me a sec."

He pressed his cheek to hers. "Lying down should help. Leave things to me."

Trusting men wasn't something she did easily but couldn't deny him or herself.

He directed her onto the table and helped her to lie on his jacket.

Her hair fell away from her face. Despite the humid night, stars twinkled brightly above. They reminded Becca of her navel jewelry.

The delicate trinkets slid over her belly.

Eric lifted her arms above her head and positioned them as though she were a ballet dancer, exhibiting her nudity to him.

Something inside her turned over.

He arranged two chairs so she could rest her feet on the backs, her legs spread widely apart. "I really like your shoes." He touched her sandal straps and polished toenails.

She giggled softly. "That tickles."

"Want me to stop?"

"No."

He traced each toe then leaned down, their mouths a breath away. "Why didn't you wear those chains around your ankle like you did at the office? What happened to your toe rings?"

Constance had warned Becca not to wear them, since they weren't really her. The fuck they weren't. Eric liked them, too. She bet her usual makeup wouldn't have bothered him either. "That stuff didn't match my dress."

"Seriously? That's the only reason?" His mouth twisted in a pout. "You should have worn them."

She would next time. Except there wouldn't be a repeat, since this was a test run for the real deal. Him conquering awesome babes. That should have encouraged her to flee because she was better than accepting crumbs from any man.

With Eric, Becca needed to enjoy whatever he could give her. Already, this evening was more than she'd hoped for. "Sorry."

"Not your fault. You didn't know how much I like them. Now, you do." He struggled to loosen his tie, gave up and shoved the ends into his shirt to keep them put. "No stopping for anything, right?"

She shook her head, obedient to whatever he willed. Not even a SWAT team and the bitching from their respective families would have convinced Becca to deny herself this. "Bring. It. On."

Grinning wolfishly, he folded her skirt back inch by inch, as he would a longed-for gift he didn't want to unwrap too quickly and relished the parts he exposed. Calves. Thighs. Pussy.

Her perfume mingled with Italian spices wafting from the restaurant, and the breeze tinged with a briny odor from the Gulf. The air whispered over her puffy folds, confirming how much damper she'd become.

Rather than play with her clit, Eric draped the skirt above her navel and fingered her stars.

Her tummy quivered. Her caution rose.

Since she'd lost her virginity at twenty, Becca had never been exposed physically to a man for a prolonged period, such as strutting her stuff in his apartment or hers as they discussed their respective days, having breakfast nude, dallying in the shower. Her hookups had always been frantic, fueled by intense loneliness, too much booze and ended up being short-lived. The proverbial wham-bam-thank-you-ma'am. Not unlike her and Eric's first go-round in the treatment room.

That had been nothing like this. He took his time, savoring each moment, eager to drink her in.

She found his attention exhilarating and daunting.

Although shadows smoothed out her many flaws, there was enough light for him to study her most intimate parts.

He quit toying with her jewelry and stroked her reddish curls.

Pleasure raged through her, along with deep-felt emotions she'd buried long ago to avoid being hurt. Instead, she'd settled on a life without intimacy and desire. Even though it was impossible for her to resist those feelings now, given what he was doing, she squeezed her fists to maintain control.

He wound a curl around his finger then tugged gently and teasingly. "Your real color?"

She barely had enough air to speak. "Uh-huh."

A crazed sound thick with passion tore from him. "Lift your ass."

Once she had, Eric cupped her cheeks, his strength keeping her elevated. He licked her cleft.

She shivered.

He sucked her.

Becca gripped the table as she would the safety bar on a rollercoaster, defending against its perilous dips and sways. This was far more dangerous and thrilling.

After lapping her juices, he tongued her clit.

Riotous feelings, along with heat she'd never known, surged through her. She shuddered.

He increased his pace.

Delight sparked from her head to her toes, feral in its intensity. Other pleasure was so new and astonishing she had to grit her teeth to keep from crying out and bringing anyone back here. In the relative quiet, too much noise drifted from the parking lot. Cars starting and stopping, voices raised in conversation or laughter. Everyone having a great time.

She pitied them for not experiencing what she did.

Tension built deep within her sheath. An itch she couldn't scratch that Eric kept tormenting her with. He licked fast, slow, medium, around her nub, on the damn thing, seemingly unable to make up his mind, wanting to drive her fucking mental, not allowing her to peak.

Each time Becca came close, he changed tactics, behaving like the bad boy he'd become.

If she didn't do something fast, she'd go nuts. With no other choice, she lifted her hips and followed his tongue.

He stroked the furrow between her cheeks and circled her anus.

A sound burst out that didn't resemble anything human or immortal. She wasn't sure she made it and worried about night critters — vamps, weres, even a possessed dog.

No one was around.

Sweaty and panting, she closed her eyes.

Eric growled and went at her like no man ever had. He pleasured her uber-sensitive clit and probed her other opening, giving her a one-in-a-zillion thrill.

She clutched the table, clenched her teeth and literally dug in her heels.

Her climax hit with hurricane force.

A horn blared.

Unless she'd shrieked. She wasn't sure and clenched her teeth to keep quiet. Oddly enough, having to be silent aroused her more. Warmth rolled over her, draining her energy, and left her struggling for air.

Gasping wasn't in the cards. She didn't have the strength and wasn't certain she'd breathe normally again. The stars spun above her as they would if she were on a carnival ride at the county fair. Her legs and arms felt leaden. Even if she'd wanted to move, she couldn't have managed it.

Eric released her ass and pushed her knees to her chest so he could go at her again.

At this rate, he was going to kill her. Needing a chance to settle down from her first orgasm, she rolled her head from side to side and pounded the table.

"Hey." He grabbed her wrists, stopping her. "You want someone to come back here and end this?"

She wasn't that loony. "Sorry."

"S'okay. But keep quiet, please."

Like a good girl, she surrendered, her limbs as limp as overcooked spaghetti, her mouth gaping like a fish smothering in air.

Eric soldiered on and loved her nub. He tunneled two fingers into her channel, imprisoning and stretching her for his awesome cock.

The pressure was delicious, her next climax a mere scream away.

Before she could plummet over the edge, he released her right knee. Beneath the ringing in her ears, faint zipping sounded. His clothes rustled.

Through it all, he sucked her clit then stopped.

A mortal couldn't have approached and seen them. Worse, they couldn't be watching. Holy crap, it could be Desi.

Becca pushed to her elbows. She and Eric were still alone. His cock protruded between his shirt tails, the column thick, rigid and even longer than it had been in the treatment room. She wanted to believe his super-stud arousal was because of her, not the potion.

Her hunger for him said the reason shouldn't matter. Her heart whispered that it would.

Ignoring her nagging doubts, she returned his gaze, unable to look anywhere else.

He winked.

She blushed like an untried virgin then got bold and drew her tongue over her lips the same as the pretty girl who'd flirted with him earlier.

Eric smiled at Becca as he hadn't Ms. Nympho and dug in his pocket. "Give me a sec to put this on."

He ripped the condom packet so fast and hard the rubber flew out, soared and dropped to the concrete on a wet plop.

Eric swore beneath his breath. "I've got more in my car. Hang tight."

He couldn't be serious. She was half-naked, spread wide and hornier than she'd ever been. "Don't leave."

She wrapped her legs around his lean hips to make certain he didn't and held tighter than she should but as much as she craved. "You don't need them." She might have been abstinent, but wasn't foolish enough to believe her resolve would last forever. "I'm protected."

Against everything except falling for him.

His grin almost touched his ears. Going in raw was the ultimate adventure for most guys. With a male's unashamed delight, he lifted his cock and bathed the plump head in her slick juices.

The pleasure he created felt better than an all-day massage and gorging on a dozen molten lava cakes. Becca wanted to witness his luscious rod burrowing into her, but her arms gave out. She sank to the table and capitulated, a willing sacrifice to him impaling her.

"Ready?" He stroked her clit, his touch light and feathery.

Her scalp tingled. She arched her back. "Oh, yeah." She was overdue.

He entered her slowly. His crown strained against her tight pussy.

She flexed her inner muscles to welcome him.

Gratitude welled in his eyes followed by hard lust. He penetrated deeper, furthering his intimate invasion, making certain her channel sheltered him.

He shouldn't have had any doubt she'd do so.

All her life, Becca had felt lonely when it came to men. During this small slice of time, she knew what it was like to have someone who was hers alone. Interested in the woman she was, liking what he saw, eager to share conversation and laughter then topping it off with precious intimacy.

That could change in a minute or a second. Warning bells went off again. She dismissed them.

On a quiet grunt, Eric pushed fully inside. His balls smacked her ass.

A marvelous feeling, but she wanted him closer and held out her arms.

He kissed her palms and positioned her arms above her shoulders, "Don't move."

"At all?" She stopped squeezing his cock with her cunt. "Sure you want that?"

His shoulders shook with laughter. "Behave."

"Are you certain you want that?"

"Let me put it to you this way. Keep your arms where they are or else."

"Or else what?"

"You won't get this." He flexed his rod then pulled her stretchy halter top to each side and exposed her boobs.

Never had Becca been as grateful she hadn't worn a bra.

Eric fondled her the way a man does when denied a woman's flesh too long. He dragged his thumbs over her nipples, cupped her breasts and rested his head between them.

His hair bore a pleasant botanical scent from his shampoo. The fragrance couldn't compete with his natural musk.

The noises he made betrayed his brutal need. His cock grew even harder within her pussy. On a strained sigh, he latched onto her nipple and sucked.

His wet heat registered everywhere, even her freaking eyelashes. This was way better than she'd dreamed or read about in erotic romances.

He flicked his tongue against her erect tip and sucked hard enough to curl her hair.

She tensed from too much pleasure and wilted at the resulting joy.

When she was at her most vulnerable, he resumed stroking her nub. Lazily. Maddeningly. Stopping and starting.

She twisted beneath him, the mounting and waning rapture too much to bear. "Let me come. Please."

He nuzzled her neck and gave her an openmouthed kiss there. Her second greatest pleasure zone.

Delight slammed into her. Unable to resist, she rode the wave, not caring about anything except having a great time.

His powerful thrusts proved the beast he'd become. He was more than sure of himself. He was damned certain of her, knowing she loved this. Each time he plowed into her, Becca's breasts jiggled. The stars spun from her soaring dizziness.

She defied his earlier order not to move and gripped his arms, needing them for support.

Eric pumped faster, identical to how he rubbed her clit. Demanding that she come.

Becca fought him, reluctant for the act to end. She distracted herself with noises coming from the lot. Hungry people arriving. Stuffed patrons departing.

He stroked and thrust repeatedly.

Perspiration slipped from her temples to her neck. Her muscles screamed from being too tense. She couldn't think or breathe. He'd reduced her to a hot mess.

He wasn't doing much better. His complexion had darkened from passion. His eyes bordered on wild.

He swooped down and kissed her. Not with brutal need but stunning tenderness. Precisely what she needed in order to let go and trust what might happen next.

She peaked.

His tongue muffled her jarring cry, allowing only her rough breaths to escape. None conveyed the pure wonder she'd experienced.

Eric broke their kiss and let loose, thrusting for all he was worth. The table tapped the concrete. Becca's elbows and shoulders rapped the top. He propped her calf on his shoulder for greater access to her cunt.

Porn stars would have loved her wanton position. She adored it too and fell even harder for him.

Sweat dotted his forehead. He looked like he might die but lasted a bit longer. His shudder, grunt and a restrained hiss announced his climax.

Before he passed out, Becca pulled her leg down and gathered him to her, her pussy still pulsing around his cock.

He lifted his head.

She expected him to say something. Not a thank you, exactly. Bad boys didn't do that. Maybe he wanted her to scoot over so he could lie down. "What?"

He slanted his mouth over hers.

Wasn't enough.

Although Eric was dead on his feet and trembling like a whipped mutt, he wanted more. He wasn't about to stop tonight, tomorrow, the next day or ever.

Becca would have to understand.

He certainly couldn't tell her how he felt, not with his mouth on hers and his tongue speared deep. She tasted like the steak and wine they'd enjoyed and something unique to her. Smoky and titillating.

Unable to get close enough, he repositioned his mouth repeatedly.

She followed his gyrations as though her life depended upon it.

His did. Eric hadn't a clue what was driving him. Even as a teen with his first conquest, he hadn't been this horny. And he'd had a damn good reason then considering his raging hormones. As a man, he was used to sex...though not with Becca. Being with her in every way was like a fixation that wouldn't let go and kept mounting in intensity. He couldn't figure it out. Didn't want to. All that mattered was having more.

With his weary cock still inside her cunt, he straightened and pulled her up with him.

"You taste good." He kissed her deeper than he ever had. His bottom teeth dug into his lip, possibly drawing blood. Eric didn't care. This was worth it.

He went at Becca until they were both breathless.

She sagged to one elbow. Her breasts bounced with each gasp.

He'd worn her out. Pleased, he kissed her lightly. "Let's make you comfortable."

Once he'd released his cock from her, he pushed his pants and underwear to his ankles and helped her off the table. "Don't move. Definitely don't leave."

She laughed quietly. "As if."

He liked her answer and dropped into a chair. "Come here."

She regarded his lap. "You want me to straddle you?"

That would have been awesome, but the chair had arms. He suspected she wasn't a contortionist any more than he was. "Sit on my lap. Your back to my front."

With a breathy sigh, she settled in.

"Good?" For him, this was paradise. He cupped her breasts and thumbed her nipples.

She sagged into him then twisted around. Her lips moved, but no words came out.

A good thing. Footfalls rang on the concrete. Couldn't be Desi—he lumbered rather than walked. This sounded like a younger guy. Maybe a server, checking to see what animal had moaned back here.

Becca didn't bother covering herself. She thrust her tongue in his mouth.

The footfalls stopped.

Eric refused to stop sucking her tongue, but he did open one eye.

No one watched them.

Metal struck metal with a loud clanging noise. Possibly from a trash container.

Whatever it was, the footfalls receded and relieved him from having to floor the guy then take off at a run with Becca. Relying on her magic to fix things wasn't an option.

She snuggled closer.

Hell, she could be the lousiest witch since time began. This was all he needed. He pulled his mouth from hers. "Stand up."

"No. I'm comfortable. Why?"

"To get more comfortable, if you get my drift."

"I do." On her feet, she lifted her dress and slung the skirt over one shoulder, hitting his eye.

He gasped.

"What happened?" She looked over and winced. "Did I hurt you?"

"Nope." He blinked wildly. "Go on. Don't make me wait. If you do, I might die."

Muted laughter jiggled her shoulders. "Don't worry. I'll give you CPR."

He was counting on it and a whole lot more. God, he loved how she horsed around, like guys did but with the added temptation of being female.

With as much skill as he might have used, she cradled his cock and brought it back to life.

The last time he'd been this hard this fast was in middle school.

She twisted around to lick his earlobe. "Ready?"

"Always."

"Careful, you don't want to get a big head."

"Too late. I already have one."

She snickered. "That you do."

Her praise made his cock grow even more. He was so damn hard, his crown demanded entrance and slipped into her easily. She took him in on a prolonged sigh, her cunt sinking down his rod until her ass and their thighs touched.

"Wow." She dropped her head.

Eric battled for restraint. An impossible fight given her sheath hugging his cock. Her inner heat surrounded him, demanding he come. He couldn't. He had to go the distance and beyond. With all the discipline he owned, Eric saw to her needs, not his. He kissed her neck and shoulder, squeezed her breasts and stroked her clit. Unable to decide which part he had to touch next he floundered, distracted by her warmth, scent and curves.

She took up the slack, pushing up to release his rod then burying it again within her juicy slit. Becca was unbelievably narrow, deliciously hot and wonderfully wet. He tugged his hair to maintain control and didn't care if he pulled out every strand. Her mom surely had a potion to fix that. She'd certainly grown enough hair on him the last time.

He didn't want to dwell on the horrible, only the good — Becca doing miraculous things to him, playing with his balls even as she rode his shaft long and hard.

He had to help. He should. That's what a nice guy would do.

If she wanted that. He still didn't know.

Worried, he rubbed her clit.

She stilled. Air whistled through her teeth.

Okay, she liked that. All women did. He kept it up.

They worked each other into a lust-filled frenzy. The chair legs scraped the concrete. She mumbled something that sounded like a prayer of thanks.

Eric answered with a groan that said this was un-fucking-believable.

They came together, grasped each other, rocked back and forth and made noises only lovers should hear.

With one final, shattering gasp, Becca collapsed against him.

Eric wound his arms around her waist and tried to calm down but failed. "Let's get out of here. My place is a couple of miles away."

Of course, her business was even closer, hopefully closed and empty at this hour.

Chapter Nine

Before she'd arrived at the restaurant, Becca had hoped to keep her head on straight and remember her purpose in being with him, rather than turning the evening into a romantic fantasy.

Yet here she was flushed from too many staggering climaxes, hair messy, makeup possibly ruined, limbs sprawled.

Delight and unease battered her in equal measure.

In the past, she'd understood and accepted that her few hookups were measured in minutes, not days, and certainly not years. They were about temporary relief, not relationships. With their passion sated, the immortals she'd slept with had grown quiet, planning their escape to avoid real intimacy or her wanting another date.

One warlock had cut out so fast, he'd left his car keys on her dresser. Rather than return to retrieve his property, the things had flown out of her bedroom window on their own. She'd hung over the sill to follow their journey. Avoiding her gaze, he'd caught his keys, fired up his pickup and zoomed away.

She'd been foolish enough to ask the next guy, a were, if he wanted to go to a concert with her the following weekend. They'd been in bed at the time, still panting from their mediocre lovemaking. Not that she was one to complain. Beggars can't be choosers and all that. She'd figured his drowsiness would weaken his defenses and he might say yes.

He'd scratched his hairy belly, grabbed his smartphone and brought up Google. After a quick search, he tapped the screen. "Nope. Full moon that night."

From her vantage point, it had looked more like a crescent moon. "That's okay. My service can fix you up with treatments to battle your urges or industrial-strength sunglasses so you can go out during the worst times without succumbing to your beastly urges. The therapy and shades are free. My treat."

He'd declined.

She wasn't certain which pissed her off more — that he didn't like her as a woman or he'd turned up his nose at her service.

Back then, she'd believed if any man offered the promise for more, she could have relaxed and been herself. A tender kiss and gentle caress would have had her soaring for weeks, even months.

Eric cradled her, his arm around her waist, hand on her breast. He rocked them in an X-rated version of comfort and care. He hadn't fled. Hell, his cock was still inside her, and he wanted to take her to his place.

She should have been doing backflips. The truth and reality about this evening precluded such joy. Fighting sadness, she stroked his fingers.

He rested his chin on her shoulder and yawned sloppily.

She smiled, even as tears stung her eyes.

Eric smacked his lips. "I'm not tired."

Of course, he wasn't. He was a newly minted beast, with better endurance than an adult film star who kept going and going on camera, that passion no more real than this night. Her heart cramped so hard the pain stole her breath. "Let me up."

"In a sec." He rubbed his nose against her neck and gave it a wet kiss.

His tongue tickled her. She wiggled.

Eric tightened his hold to keep her still and close.

Becca sought his mouth, lost in the moment too easily, and had no excuse, except that she was only human, or partially so, and painfully weak when it came to him. She yearned for Eric, at least the real Eric, the same way her parents still longed for each other.

This wasn't anywhere close to what they had.

After their fateful first meeting, her parents had grown close the mortal way. Rowena didn't have to use any love spells or potions on Wade. He'd craved her from the beginning, as she had him, their bond magical — more powerful than any sorcery.

Becca had always wanted that for herself yet had ended up with so little.

Eric ended their kiss and pressed his cheek to hers. His skin was smooth and hot, scented with his aftershave and her fragrance. She ached to throw her arms around him in an honest, impassioned caress, but didn't. Couldn't.

He played with her nipple. "Are you falling asleep?"

She wished. Doing so, while being sheltered within his embrace, would have been awesome. Then she wouldn't have to consider the inevitable. With it weighing down on her, she shook her head.

"Sure?" He slid his hand from her breast to her ribs. "You're awfully quiet."

"No, I'm not—what are you doing?"

"What do you think?"

She pressed her face to her shoulder to mute her giggles. "Don't! I'm ticklish!"

"You think?"

A husky laugh erupted from her. She tugged his fingers. He kept tickling her. She tried to slap his hand away and finally clawed him.

Didn't faze Eric at all.

Becca convulsed with laughter, her face lifted to the sky, throat exposed.

He trailed kisses on her neck.

She panted like a contented dog.

"Can you walk to my car?" He pecked her jawline. "Or do you need me to carry you?"

She tightened her cunt around his cock. A risky move she couldn't resist, though she warned herself not to go further. "Give me a sec."

"Take all the time you want. What you're doing feels great."

His strained breathing sounded as turned on as hers did. His shaft stiffened within her.

Knowing where this would lead, and where it wouldn't, she stopped squeezing him and tried to stand but couldn't. Desire weakened her. "We can't stay here all night."

He said something beneath his breath and pressed his mouth to her ear. "Okay, I'll carry you to my car."

"No."

He stilled. "Why not? I don't mind. Don't you think I'm capable?"

"I know you are, but it's not necessary."

"If we want to get from here to there it might be."

Becca wanted to be straight with him, but couldn't bring herself to do so. Uneasy, she came up with the best excuse she could manage. "With a flick of my hand, I can send you wherever you want to go."

Eric leaned around to meet her gaze and made a face. "You mean magic?"

His misgiving didn't surprise Becca. She was doomed to be a shitty witch and didn't care. "Guess I'll walk."

He stroked her arm.

She went limper than she had been.

"Sure you want to hoof it?" He kissed her biceps. "I don't want you getting tired. At least not until we're somewhere private. Your office is nearby. It's closed for the night, isn't it?"

The heat from his words and breath traveled to Becca's core and landed deep within her soul. "Ah, no. We don't shut down until dawn, at least the night crew. That's when the day crew takes over. We have to do two twelve-hour shifts. It's murder for overtime, but our weres like to come in during the day, for the most part. Vamps have appointments all evening for the obvious reasons."

"Right. I forgot about that. Them." He hugged her. "My condo it is."

She had to stop this now. "My place is in the French Quarter, a block up from my business."

"Sounds good."

"I could walk from here. It's not that far away."

Eric gave her an odd look. "You want to walk?"

Becca wasn't certain she could. She'd never been as weary, not even when guys had dumped her with shameful disregard. However, getting in his car wasn't in the equation either. She'd make more excuses that would prolong the pain.

"What's wrong?" His smile wobbled the way it does when a man isn't certain his chain's being yanked or not. "You can't be worried that I've had too much to drink to get behind the wheel. I had less wine than you."

Becca knew what she had to say, but couldn't get the words out.

"Oh, hey." He grew ultra serious. "You think I'm too tired to drive because of this?" He gestured to their partially naked state, the fact that his cock was still inside her sheath.

She shrugged. "Maybe."

"But walking through a crowd of drunken tourists, dodging their elbows and feet will perk me up?" He gave her a look that said she'd lost her mind. "I'll drive."

She needed to say something and put an end to this.

The words wouldn't come.

"Up you go." He helped Becca to her feet.

She missed having him inside her. A truth she'd have to get used to.

He offered her his handkerchief. The clean linen smelled like fabric softener and had been ironed, too. He knew how to turn a girl's head. The other guys she'd been with would have given her a used napkin or her own clothes, if they'd even thought to consider her needs.

Sorrow crept more deeply inside her. She tidied up as best she could.

He did the same and dressed. With his jacket slung over one shoulder, Eric offered her his free hand.

To accept it was beyond wrong.

She did, anyway.

He kissed her fingertips.

Her longing for him grew exponentially.

On the way to his car, his step was more than light. He was wired again, ready for round two.

Given the potion he'd taken, Becca wasn't surprised.

He helped her inside his Benz and drove to the French Quarter, his hand planted on her knee, his touch assured and possessive.

For tonight. As far as tomorrow was concerned, she didn't want to go there.

He squeezed her knee. "Where do you live?"

"Not far." She pointed at a car leaving a parking space. "Pull over there."

"Why?" He looked out her window at the departing vehicle. "Isn't there parking at your place?"

"Not always. Go—now—before someone else grabs it."

After several tries, he jockeyed his car into the tight spot.

Horns screeched behind them.

Couples in their twenties and thirties passed, laughing hysterically. They held beer bottles between their thumbs and forefingers. Across the street, a sax and trumpet wailed, the sounds mournful. Horse hooves clip-clopped. A mare passed, pulling a white carriage. The lovers in the backseat kissed passionately. To them no one else existed.

Becca wanted to curl up in a ball and die. Being a coward, she hugged her purse to her chest. "You can leave me here."

"What?"

She opened her door lock.

"What are you doing? Wait." Eric captured her wrist. "You actually think I'd leave you here? Why would I do that?"

For them, it was the only sensible solution.

He glanced out of the windshield as she did. From where they were, her office roof and balcony were visible.

He stared at them then her. "You're going back to work? Now?"

She was going to find the closest bar, knock back several whiskeys to dull her heartache and drag home.

He swore beneath his breath. "Becca, I asked you a question. Answer me."

She said what she had to, not what she wanted. "The evening's over, Eric. I'm going home." She forced herself to look at him. Her heart sank at his confusion and frustration but she wouldn't glance away. At the very least, she owed him eye contact. "I'm doing that alone."

His mouth fell open.

If she'd confessed to being a man who'd had a sex change, she probably couldn't have surprised him more.

"What in the fuck is this about? What did I do? Tell me."

"You didn't do anything."

"Screw that. I must have or you wouldn't be taking off."

This was too hard. She'd always been on the side he was on now, trying to figure out why guys didn't want her. She had no skills in being the one doing the dumping. "This is nothing more than the night coming to an end and you going your way while I go mine."

"You mean like people do on blind dates when they hate the person they're with? They offer polite goodbyes then sighs of relief when it's over? Is that what you're saying?"

"No."

"So, our time together wasn't that bad, but it wasn't good enough for you to stick around. Is that what you're saying? You can't wait to cut out because you don't want to prolong the pain, even if it's on the mild side?" Astonishment crossed his features. His mood turned pensive then pissed. "Uh-uh. I don't believe that. No matter what you say, I'll never believe that you had a lousy time."

"Of course, I didn't. It was great from beginning to end, except for right now. Tonight was probably the best night of my life."

He nodded unsurely. "That sounds good."

"It isn't." She pulled her wrist from him. "Don't you understand? It's not real."

"What isn't?"

This night, what they'd done together, how they behaved, especially him. Her soul yearned for a genuine romance. Love in endless supply that she'd never get. Before she got to the restaurant, Becca had tried to convince herself a wonderful evening was all she needed. She knew better now. Being with him even on a fake date made her want more. She should have told him that but didn't have the guts. More importantly, she didn't want a guy she had to convince or use magic on even if it came from her mom.

"What's going on with you?" He searched her face. "You were eager as hell back at Desi's. Now you're acting like we barely know each other and what you do know about me you don't like."

"That's not it."

"Then dammit what is? Tell me."

"Fine." She slammed her purse against the center console. "Quit pretending tonight was more than a dry run for the real thing to test your beastly prowess. What you and I shared wasn't a freaking date. Not. Even. Close."

Shock then offense sped over his face. "You've got to be kidding."

Becca crossed her arms and leaned against her door. "Okay, let's talk about what really happened tonight. Every freaking minute."

"I don't have to. I. Was. There." He pushed his shoulder into his door. "I thought you were, too. Apparently, I was wrong. You were only pretending to laugh, horse around, share your past, sleep with me and enjoy yourself. Wow, you're quite the actress. Have you ever considered relocating to Hollywood? They could really use you out there."

She gritted her teeth. "No matter what you think, I didn't fake one laugh."

"How about your orgasms? You had four — no, five. I was counting."

As a guy, he would. "What do you think?"

"I don't know. Why don't you tell me? Make my night complete."

"Sex isn't always about you."

His face got red. "Then you didn't come? Is that it?"

"Hell, no it isn't!" She shouted as loudly as he did. "I didn't fake one damn climax."

"Neither did I."

Becca tightened her arms and fists. "That's not the point."

His eyes widened. "Then what the hell is?"

"Have you ever behaved with other women as you did with me tonight?"

He stared then pressed against his door as a trapped animal would. "Why?"

"Eric."

He muttered something. "No, I haven't behaved with any woman as I have with you. Dammit, Becca, you really turn me on. If you think I'm going to apologize for that then you're out of your pissing mind. I like you. Everything about you. Except for this weird conversation."

"The potion's making you aroused. Not me."

"What? No. That's nuts. I don't believe it."

He was worse than her, refusing to face the truth. "How do you feel now?"

"Shitty." He hunched over. "You?"

"Eric, how do you feel? Exactly?"

"Hurt. Confused. Frustrated. Horny. All right? But that doesn't mean squat." He shoved his hair off his forehead. "The potion was supposed to bring out my inner beast and turn me into a bad boy, not make me want you."

"I know, and it did the bad boy part."

His anger collapsed into concern. "You don't like that?"

He was killing her. She didn't know whether to scream at him or soothe his doubt. "Of course, I do. The way you behaved tonight was beyond wonderful. You were freaking great."

He grinned. "Yeah?"

Before he got too thrilled, she pressed on. "But that wasn't the only thing the potion did."

He looked at his groin. "It made me too big? I hurt you?"

Rubbing her temple, she struggled not to laugh or sigh. "No. Again, you're perfect."

Boundless pride flickered in his eyes.

She hated to kill his feel-good buzz but didn't have a choice. "The potions weren't mine, remember? My mom chose the ingredients. She wasn't all that certain how you'd react to the second one after what happened with the first. She'd never worked on a god before. Clearly, the potions did stuff you never asked for."

Understanding dawned on his face. "That's crap. Just because you don't think any guy is going to want you doesn't mean your mother cast a fucking spell on me so I would."

Becca's cheeks burned, her dignity a distant memory. Her only hope now was that their argument wouldn't take too much longer. "Your attraction to me could very well be collateral damage."

"You're saying what you and I did tonight, the way we kissed, made love and all the other good stuff in between was no more than collateral damage?"

"I'm saying it's a result of magic. How the potions acted separately and combined. It could have been innocent or deliberate."

He leaned away. "Now, it's a plot? Who are you?"

A woman he should never have met. Becca would never forgive herself for fucking him up as she had. He'd been perfect. Now, he was more uncertain and hurt than he'd been when he came to the service. "My mom worries about me, okay? Could be she got tired of seeing me lonely and saw her chance to fix that with you. I'm not blaming her. I'm simply calling this what it is. A sham."

He blinked. "You're not going to see me again, are you?"

Tears welled in her eyes. "You deserve better. So do I."

Eric gestured frantically. "What in the fuck is that supposed to mean?"

"I need a guy who wants me. Only me." She tried not to sound shrill but couldn't help it. "I want to be able to be myself, which means full-figured and plain, without having to worry about every woman stealing him."

"Don't you mean me? Now you're accusing me of being unfaithful? Tell me one time, just once tonight, that I looked at another woman."

He hadn't. That wasn't real, either. "You didn't. Thanks to the potion."

"Fuck that. I didn't because I didn't want to. What man would if he was with you? You're gorgeous. Your figure's to die for."

Praise she'd been waiting her entire life to hear. Too bad it came from a potion rather than his heart. Her throat constricted. She cleared it. "I'm trying to be a realist here, okay? The only way I'm going to have a future with a guy is if he falls in love with who I am, how I look, my good points and my flaws."

"Dammit, you don't have any."

"Yeah, that's realistic." She pinched her nose. "Listen to yourself. The magic's talking, not you."

He turned away, giving her the proverbial cold shoulder, his attention on the street scene, everyone drunk and happy.

Becca envied them.

"This isn't about what your mother did or didn't do." He squeezed the steering wheel. "You tried me out and for reasons unknown to me, I didn't pass your test."

"There was no test. Look at me."

He rested his forehead against his window. "No."

"Please."

He faced her. Hurt and bewilderment played across his features.

Becca's heart pounded worse than it had earlier. "Nothing you did tonight impressed me more than the first moment we met. I liked you then. I still do."

He looked even more confused. "So you're saying you don't like the new me, after all? A few minutes ago, you said you did. Which is it?"

"I enjoyed it, but it's not real."

"The fuck it isn't. Let me finish." He held up his hand to keep her from interrupting. "The magic didn't make me sprout wings or a thirty-inch cock. This is me. You'd know that if we kept going out. We could see where this takes us."

"No, we can't."

"Why? Afraid to find out that our chemistry has nothing to do with the stupid potion?"

Becca knew it couldn't be anything else. No man, certainly none as sinfully handsome as him, with an awesome sense of humor and a good heart, had ever fallen for her. In two days, no less.

"Trust me, it is." She lifted her chin and forced herself to be strong. "I know you don't believe me, so test it out yourself. Ask someone out. See what happens. I'm not wrong."

"You want me to go on a date?" He made a derisive noise. "If I'm obsessed with you because of your mother's magic, won't being with another woman prove to be kind of pointless? Won't that be unfair to the other woman?"

Of course, it would, but who said life was fair? It sure as hell kept screwing up her happiness. "It's one date. Surely, no woman will fall that quickly."

"Like you?"

His bald statement and the sorry truth behind it sent heat to Becca's face. Yeah, she'd fallen for him at blinding speed and would simply have to get over it. "Maybe your Uncle Desi put something in my food. Could be he put something in yours, too, which only exacerbated the problem."

"So, you're admitting you fell for me tonight. The new me, the old me, some part of me. Take your pick. Just don't deny it."

She couldn't say anything at all.

Eric leaned across the console and got in her face. "How often have you behaved with another man as you did with me tonight?"

Never, not even when she'd been horny and drunk. "You need to tell your uncle not to play with magic."

"Sure, you go with the fantasy that he and your mom caused this, not the truth of what you're honestly feeling. Whatever helps you sleep at night."

"I'm sorry, Eric. I didn't plan for this to happen."

He leaned away and wouldn't look at her.

Becca wanted to console him except the right words didn't exist. She opened her door. The car ding-ding-dinged. The crowd laughed and hollered. Music played. She wanted to shriek.

"I thought you were leaving." He looked over. "No, wait. That came out wrong. Go on and leave. I'm tired of this shit."

Becca hated ending things with him this way. This wasn't his fault. He'd only wanted a little happiness, the same as everyone else. Too bad he'd pursued magic to get it. There should have been a black box warning on every potion and spell rather than advertisements trying to hawk more to unsuspecting fools. "I'll talk to my mom. Get her to cancel out whatever she did to you. That way, you can get on with your life. Don't change anything about yourself, Eric. You're perfect. Always have been. You're the most wonderful man I've ever met."

She hurried from his car and ran down the street.

Eric had no idea what the fuck had happened. Even after dating thousands of women who couldn't break up quickly enough, Becca had blindsided him in a way he couldn't have predicted. For the first time in his life, he wished he was nonsexual. Maybe there was a potion or spell for that. He yanked off his seat belt and scrambled out of his vehicle. "Becca!"

She tore down the street, darting between people.

"Becca!"

She disappeared in a sea of humanity.

Her red hair flashed.

Eric rushed toward her and stopped. The color wasn't her hair but a scarf wrapped around a woman's head so she could look like a medium or some other freaky thing.

He bounced in place, wanting her to move the fuck away.

She did.

The crowd parted, providing a better view of what lay ahead. Becca was already gone, ducked into a shop, bar or restaurant, unless she'd disappeared in a puff of smoke.

She couldn't be that reckless, considering she wasn't a great witch.

Eric followed for several yards until he remembered his car doors were open, his keys in the ignition. Spell, his ass. Potion, his butt. If her mother had done something weird to him, he wouldn't be worrying about his Benz being snatched.

He returned to it. A guy he'd never seen before sat in the passenger seat, guzzling whatever was in his Styrofoam cup.

"Out." Eric grabbed the guy's arm and hauled him from the seat.

"Hey man." He jerked away. "I saw this baby first."

"The baby belongs to me." Eric bared his teeth. "Want to make something of it?" A suicidal question. The guy had fifty pounds or better on him, most in lard and a lot settled in his huge fists.

"Nope." He lifted his hands in surrender. "You have a nice night."

That wasn't fucking likely. He slammed Becca's door, climbed into his seat and spent too much time trying to pull out of the puny space. Horns blared. He leaned on his own, traded oaths with passing motorists and sweated worse than a damn pig. Once he maneuvered onto the street, he glanced at the passing bars, restaurants and businesses, determined to scour each.

The traffic wouldn't let him slow down. There was no damn place to park.

He didn't care and stopped yards from her business. The lights were on. A shadow that didn't resemble anything human rushed across a window and slammed into the glass. The shutters shook. Someone, possibly Zoe, hauled whatever it was away.

Eric tapped his thumbs against his steering wheel. If Becca had fled to her office, he should follow and reason with her.

What he'd felt tonight couldn't have been the potion or potions. That was beyond ludicrous. From the moment she'd ordered him to strip and asked if he wore baggy boxers, he'd liked her. She was bossy as hell, fun, honest and sweet, when she wanted to be. She was also intelligent and so fucking unsure of herself she'd loused up the best thing that had come her way.

Namely, him.

He should go up there and confront her. If that was coming on too strong, he could call her from his car phone, after he blocked his number so she'd pick up. The best choice might be to give her space until tomorrow. Let her cool off and reconsider what she'd said and thought. Give her a chance to miss him as he did her.

His chest was so tight he couldn't breathe. His ears rang. Losing her was like dying.

He had to see her right now, this fucking minute, and get her to talk to him. Unless she said something worse than she already had. Maybe a good night's sleep would put her in a better mood.

Then again…

He cursed his indecision, idiotic potions, fucking magic, stupid powers that screwed things up rather than fixing them and all the other crap that messed up his life.

A horn blared.

Eric flinched. Growling, he gave the driver behind him the finger.

The horn shrieked again.

Reluctantly, he drove past Becca's building. With each mile, his mood grew darker, more pissed and uncertain too. What if Desi had put something in their food? Like her, he'd had the same thought, which he'd dismissed.

No more. Their damned relatives could have meddled in their time together tonight, which wasn't a date. Despite all he and Becca had shared, maybe their encounter was a test run, as he'd suggested, but only so she'd go out with him.

Not once had he considered looking for another woman. Becca was the only one who was perfect for him. Always would be.

He needed the truth and wanted to believe she desired who he was as much as he hoped she did.

And as deeply as he craved her.

Chapter Ten

"Come on, girl, make the call." Constance pushed Becca's smartphone from across the desk to between her elbows.

She leaned away from the device as she would something that might bite or kill her.

Constance tapped her foot. "It's either that or I'll put my hands on your head. Pull those nasty memories away in a flash. You'll never know what hit you. Is that what you want? Not to remember anything about him?"

Fool that she was, Becca wanted to keep her memories of Eric safe and cherished. It was the only thing she had left.

"I don't think she wants to forget." Heather clasped her knees and rocked on Becca's sofa. "Maybe she'd like to do this as a mortal would."

Zoe stopped pacing. "You mean, suffer. Put up the good fight. Endure pain like never before because it makes you a stronger and better person."

Spoken like a true missionary who wanted to sell the flock on misery. Becca figured heartache would kill her way before redemption came. She couldn't sleep, eat or think. Death couldn't be this awful.

"I wouldn't want her to be unhappy." Heather's chin trembled. "That would be awful. No, I don't want her to suffer." She spoke to Becca. "Please don't."

A tall order. "I'm trying not to." Sadly, she wasn't doing a good job. Almost a week had passed since the test run with Eric. She kept going over that night, everything he'd said and had done, looking for confirmation to support what she'd told him about the potions' effects. For the most part, she found proof. Sometimes she didn't. Those moments increased her doubt. Worse, they gave her hope. A four-letter word if ever there was one. Buoyed with longing, she rethought things and had even built an Excel spreadsheet with pros and cons detailing what happened between them. What it could mean.

She hadn't a clue what that might be, and it drove her nuts. No way could she stand another moment of this slow torture.

The office phone rang.

Becca flinched. She couldn't look at caller ID. Four times Eric had left voicemails at her extension, thanks to Heather's recorded instructions on how to reach various staff members. In his defense, he didn't have her unlisted personal number. They'd never gotten that far in their non-relationship. Hearing his deep voice had thrilled Becca and also sped her toward unrelenting gloom. He spoke calmly. She trembled. His messages were to-the-point and commanding, stating they had to talk. Of course, that was three days ago. He hadn't contacted her since then. She wanted to cry.

Heather stood. "Should I get that?"

"Looks like it, since our boss lady certainly isn't." Constance gestured Heather over.

Becca pushed into her chair. If it was Eric, she couldn't talk to him. That was too scary. She knew her limitations. If they were even in the same building, she'd cave and go the easy route, have a great time and delude herself that he wanted her for who she was. Not because the magic had changed him.

She'd avoid the inevitable end.

There was always a Dear Jane message for her from every guy she'd known. Being dumped was the only thing she was good at with men. Eric thought he'd had it hard with women. That was a joke. He was a mere baby when it came to sucking at love. Becca had it down pat.

She shouldn't have fallen so hard and fast or let what she felt for him screw with her.

For days, she feared he'd walk through the front door. He never did. That pushed her into a new tailspin filled with despair. She reasoned he hadn't come around, and wouldn't, because the potion had somehow worn off. He'd forgotten about her. He probably didn't want to tangle with her crew either. She couldn't blame him.

Heather finally reached the desk.

Becca braced herself for the worst. "I'm not here…if it's for me."

Constance lifted her gaze to the ceiling. "Who else would it be for at your extension? No, wait, don't answer that. I don't think I could follow how your mind works."

"Constance." Heather shook her head. "That's not nice. Becca needs our support."

"Hey, I agree she certainly needs something. Not necessarily us, though. Let's see who's calling." She leaned over.

Becca tensed.

"Even upside down it looks like the company that hosts the annual warlock conventions."

Her spirits nosedived. "Let it go to voicemail."

"You're sure?" Constance arched one eyebrow. "Maybe having some fun would get you out of your funk."

Unless it was with Eric, that was doubtful. "I'm good."

"If you say so. But if you get any better than you are now, we're going to have to call the suicide hotline."

Becca folded her arms on her desk, rested her head on them and called herself an idiot. After so much time and no additional phone calls from Eric, he'd given up and moved on. A wise choice. He'd saved himself future grief and spared her from having to call her mom, as she'd promised, to ask Rowena to lift whatever she'd zapped him with.

Constance ran her hand over Becca's hair.

She stiffened and shot up. "What are you doing?"

"Relax. I'm only consoling you." She made a show of lifting her hands. "My offer still stands, though. You can't go on like this. Hell, we can't, either. You're murder to work with. You need to forget him or know the truth, with that being my personal preference. Go on, call the man."

"It's only his uncle." Heather looked hopeful. "Not Eric. Maybe it won't be so bad."

Or maybe it would be awful, Desi admitting he'd spiked their food and that's what had caused such a bewitching night. Sweet, sexy memories Becca was afraid to hold onto but didn't want shattered either. Not yet. Maybe in several months or a year.

"You want me to call him?" Constance reached for the phone.

Becca pushed her hand away. "No. I want all of you to go back to work."

Heather raced to the door. Zoe blocked it and gave her a look that said, "sit down, no one's leaving". Heather drew in her shoulders. Before she fell apart, Becca gestured her back to the sofa. Constance was right. It was time to learn the horrible truth.

It'd hurt like hell, but would be the first step toward eventually growing numb then moving through each day like a zombie. Becca was glad her friends were here to support the beginning of the end. She didn't think she could do this alone.

Nauseous, she lifted her smartphone and lost her nerve. "I don't have his number."

Constance pushed Becca's notepad to her. Written across the top, in three-inch high numerals, was the reservation line for Desiderio.

"What time is it?" Becca looked at the sun, not her desk clock. "He's not open until six. It's too early. He won't be there."

"I called twenty minutes ago." Constance tapped his number. "He answered the phone. We all have a reservation for tomorrow night."

"What?" Becca pushed back in her chair so quickly, the legs bounced then scraped over the floor. "I'm not going to eat there again."

Constance lifted one shoulder. "Then the three of us will. Right, ladies?"

Heather chewed her lower lip and looked at Becca uncertainly.

The flames in Zoe's eyes flared. "Even if you do ask him what he did, how do you know he'll tell the truth? He could always lie."

Becca put down the phone.

Constance slapped it back into her hand. "Ask him in such a way that he can't lie."

"How am I supposed to do that?"

"Don't grill the man or make it sound as though you're accusing him of anything. Tell him your time there with Eric was so wonderful that you wish you could have another night like that again. You'd do anything for it."

Becca sagged in her chair. "Won't he just make another reservation for Eric and me?"

"Not if you word what you say carefully. Praise him. Pull him into your confidence. Use your womanly wiles. You do have some, don't you?"

She curled her upper lip.

"That's not the right attitude to have." Constance gave her a sour look. "Puff the man up. Make him think he's the only one who can help you with this. If he did do anything to your and Eric's food, he'll offer to do it again because you're praising him so much."

Heather nodded and smiled. "Then you'll have your answer."

Becca bared her teeth.

Heather shrank back. "Or not."

"It's either that or return Eric's calls." Constance pointed to the business phone. "Ask him how he feels."

"Uh-uh." Becca waved her hands. "Any answer he gives me could be the magic talking."

"Always a possibility. Which means that after you speak to Eric's uncle, you need to finally call your mom. Find out exactly what she put in that last potion. I know, I know." Constance inhaled deeply and sighed. "Having mixed it, you're well aware of the ingredients. However, as you've already told us, you haven't a clue how they interacted with each other or with that first potion. She does."

Zoe smoothed her plaid skirt. "Becca would, too, if she'd studied her craft a little harder and respected the magic."

Too late for that now.

Constance spoke to Becca. "If your mom did mess with it, which I don't believe at all, I'm sure she had the right intention."

Heather nodded vigorously. "Rowena's a nice lady. She only wants what's best for everyone."

Becca hoped to hell that didn't include blindsiding poor Eric into liking her daughter, unless the side effects had been an accident. Her mom had never worked on a god before. Therefore, she wouldn't have known what might ultimately happen. Not that it being accidental would make this any better. Eric's transformation in the treatment room, well before he and Becca had eaten the possibly spiked meal, had to be from the potion. And what about the way he'd acted before they'd even gone inside Desiderio's, taking her in his arms, kissing her as if there was no tomorrow, ignoring Ms. Nympho in favor of her. Yeah, that made sense. Desi might be responsible for what happened during and after their meal, but not before. Even Eric had admitted he'd never behaved with another woman as he had with her.

Becca wished she'd been born fully mortal without this other crud to worry about.

Constance rubbed her back. "Want me to punch in the number?"

"I'm capable."

"I know. So get a move on."

Becca tried twice but hit the wrong numbers. "I'm doing it, okay?" She turned her back to Constance and finally got the combination right.

The first ring sounded.

She wanted to throw up.

Desi's gravelly voice cut off the second ring. "Buona sera! Desiderio's. How can we make your life more beautiful than it already is?"

Becca wanted Eric. The real Eric. She figured that wasn't on Desiderio's menu.

"Hello?" He spoke louder. "Is anyone there?"

"Ah…"

"I'm sorry, there must be something wrong with our connection. I didn't hear that. Can you repeat it?"

Becca covered her face with her hand. "Hi. This is Becca Salt. I was there the other night? With —"

"Becca! How wonderful to hear from you. Your voice is just as lovely on the phone as it is in person. How's Eric?"

She dropped her hand. How was she supposed to know? "Ah…"

"What was that? You keep fading in and out. It's probably my phone. Let me go outside for a better connection. This happens sometimes. Just give me a second to get out there."

"No, don't." She lowered her voice and tried to sound less panicked. "The phone's fine."

"Oh, okay. You want to make a reservation for you and Eric tonight?" He chuckled. "I'll have the same table ready for you, like the last time."

Becca slumped in her chair, uncertain whether to be happy that Eric hadn't brought another woman there yet, or bummed because this was proof Desi had messed with their food. The man oozed confidence that she and Eric were into each other in every conceivable way. "No, I'm calling about something else."

Constance hurried around the desk and mouthed, "Play it cool."

Perspiration ran down Becca's back.

"Oh, you want to make reservations for another group?" Papers rustled on Desi's end. "You and the ladies you work with? A girl's night out? Someone's birthday?"

She squirmed in her chair.

Constance mouthed, "What?"

Becca shooed her away and spoke to Desi. "Ah, no. That is, I didn't call to make a reservation. I just wanted…that is…when Eric and I were there the other night…"

"Yes, yes. What?"

Becca fell silent.

Constance rolled her eyes. Heather rocked super fast on the sofa. Zoe looked smug, saying she knew this wouldn't work out.

Becca braced for the worst. "Did you put something in our food?"

Constance ground her fist into her forehead.

Desi growled. "What?"

It sounded like "back off". Becca couldn't. "Did you put something in our food? I'm not accusing you or anything."

Constance shook her head.

Becca tried to ignore her. "It's just that, well, everything was so wonderful."

Desi snorted. "That's because I'm a good cook."

"Oh, hey, I agree. Best meal I ever had. But…"

"But what?" His voice got edgier. "Did Eric put you up to this?"

"Eric? No." Becca pushed up in her chair. "What do you mean?"

"He called me earlier in the week, demanding to know whether I messed with your food that night. I kept telling him no. Not that I didn't think about it. A lot. Trust me, that boy needs help when it comes to women. He can never close the deal. But my wife said, 'You leave them alone. Let nature take its course.'" He sniffed. "As if that ever works. Now you tell Eric I don't appreciate him having you call to accuse me of nothing I didn't do, even though I should have."

Becca trembled so badly, her voice shook. "You really didn't put anything in the food? No aphrodisiac? No magic or whatever gods use? I'm half-witch, by the way, on my mom's side, so it's okay if you tell me."

"I just did. And I already knew about your background."

"How?"

"How else? I pulled it out of Eric."

That didn't sound good. "He didn't want to talk about me?"

"He couldn't talk about nothing else. For two hours, he grilled me to make sure I didn't do nothing to you. That you were too fine a girl to play with. That if I did do something, he'd never speak to me again. I told him, go on, clam up, that would give me a vacation from his problems with the ladies. He started yapping again. Becca this. Becca that. I let him talk himself out. He would have anyway."

"What exactly did he say?"

"How should I know? The ball game was on at the same time. I was listening to it. My wife said that was rude. And Eric never hearing a word I say isn't?"

"Ah…" She didn't want to get involved in a family feud, especially if it involved her. She would have killed for a recording of their conversation though. "Do you ever tape your phone calls?"

"No. Why should I?"

"Just wondering. So you're saying you honestly didn't put anything unusual in our meals?"

Constance pumped her arms in the air, making a V for victory. Heather smiled and wept. Zoe looked unconvinced.

Desi growled. "Just my secret ingredients that I'm not sharing with nobody."

"Secret ingredients." Becca's stomach fell.

So did Constance's arms. Heather pressed her hands to her chest. Zoe nodded and gave everyone an I-told-you-so look.

"Yeah." Desi made a pissed sound. "Herbs, stuff like that."

"Only herbs?" Becca's mood soared. "And simply to flavor the food?"

"Sure. Nothing supernatural, okay? What is it with you young people? You should be thanking me for a wonderful meal, not accusing me of messing with your lives. Though they do need messing with."

"Sorry. I didn't mean to accuse you of anything. I was just wondering."

"You mean Eric was. I'm gonna tell that boy if he doesn't drop this, then I'm gonna —"

"Please don't." Her blood ran cold. "It's best we forget about it, all right? Please?"

He muttered something. "What exactly happened after you two left here?"

Becca went into a full-body blush.

"No, don't tell me." He released a breath. "I don't want to know. So you really liked my food?"

"Best I ever ate, I swear."

"You didn't even try my tiramisu."

"I will the next time."

"I'm keeping you to that. When can we expect you and Eric again?"

Becca's palm sweated so much she had to wipe it and her phone off before she could answer. "I'll have to get back to you, okay?"

"Is my nephew holding a grudge against me because I served you two that night?"

She had no idea. "I can't imagine he'd do that. We, ah, haven't been back yet because there's work to do and stuff."

"You young people don't know how to have fun."

Becca wasn't crazy enough to remind him about her accusation regarding aphrodisiacs. "You're probably right."

"I know I am. Tell you what. I'll pencil you in for Saturday night. Even busy people like you and him don't work then. How's eight sound?"

Her throat tightened. "Can I get back to you on that?"

"Is Eric there with you? Is he shaking his head? Put him on, I want to talk to him."

"He's not here. I'm at work."

"Oh." Desi sounded genuinely surprised. "Well, when you two talk again, tell him that he's bringing you here at eight on Saturday. I won't take no for an answer."

Of course not, that would be too easy for her. "Okay."

"See you then, beautiful lady."

"Uh-huh. Bye." She dropped her phone and moaned.

Constance squeezed her shoulder. "Hey, girl, you got good news, right? You should be doing a happy dance."

She should have her head examined. "Can you remove my memories of that call? Just the call?"

"No way. Not until you tell me everything he said."

"Constance." Heather tried to frown. Wasn't easy for a good fairy. "Don't be mean."

"Sorry, sweetie." She spoke to Becca. "What's wrong?"

"Eric and I have reservations for Saturday night. Desi insisted upon it."

"Yeah, I know his game." Zoe planted her hands on her hips. "He's going to spike your food again."

"He didn't play with it the first time." Becca had been so certain he had. Apparently, the potions bore the total blame. "That must be what Eric wanted to talk to me about."

"Call him and find out." Constance offered Becca the phone.

She pushed it away. "There's still my mom."

"Such a nice woman." Worry crossed Heather's lovely face. "You're not going to holler at her, are you?"

Constance waved her hand. "Of course not." She spoke to Becca. "Are you?"

"No. But I do need to talk to her alone. Go back to work, please."

Heather fled the room.

Constance backed away. Her gold-and-black gown fluttered with each step. "You're sure?"

She nodded.

Zoe didn't budge from the doorway.

Becca pointed at her. "You, too."

"You heard the lady." Constance grabbed Zoe's arm and tugged her into the hall.

Smoke poured from her hair.

"Don't pull that shit on me." Constance arched one eyebrow. "I'm not impressed."

Zoe sneered. "Becca needs me to protect her."

"No, she doesn't. She's only going to call her mom." Constance spoke to Becca. "Do it. You're killing me with the suspense."

It wasn't doing her any good, either.

She closed her door and slumped against it. After several calming breaths that didn't relax her, she speed-dialed her mom.

"Baby." Warmth flowed from Rowena. "I'm so glad you called."

Renewed worry twisted Becca's insides. "Why?"

Chair legs scraped the floor.

She guessed her mom was in the kitchen and taking a load off. Good thing given what they needed to discuss.

"I'm glad you called because you're my daughter. Isn't that good enough?"

"Sure. But there's no other reason?"

Rowena made an indistinct sound. "Should there be another one?"

"I don't know. Look, Mom, I'm not accusing you of anything."

"Accusing me?" The chair legs scraped again, followed by tapping sounds. Rowena pacing. "What's going on?"

"I'm not sure. Those potions you came up with for Eric…"

"Your Roman god."

"He's not mine. What did you put in them?"

"Don't you remember?"

Becca bit back an oath. Why did everyone make having a conversation so freaking hard? "Of course, I do."

"Is there a problem?"

She dropped in her chair. "You tell me."

"Wait—has something happened to him? Is he growing hair again? Losing it?"

"I don't know. I haven't seen him for nearly a week since our date."

Rowena inhaled sharply. "You had a date? That's wonderful. Where did he take you? What did you two do? How did it go?"

"How do you think?" Becca rested her forehead on her desk. "It was magic. The best time I ever had."

"That's wonderful."

"No, it's not."

The tapping and pacing stopped. "I'm not following. Why are you so upset?"

"I know you worry about me. I know you want me to find someone."

"Well, yes, I do. Is that wrong?"

Becca couldn't get into that. It'd derail this conversation and might take several days to sort out a mother's feelings and a daughter's burden in living through them. "No, it's not wrong unless you tried to make what happened with Eric happen. I've always wanted what you and Dad have. Not magic. Not spells. The real deal."

"Eric isn't giving it to you?"

Becca gripped her desk. "I don't know. That's the problem. Please don't lie. Did you put something into that second potion to make him like me?"

"I don't understand. You're calling me because he likes you?"

"That's an understatement. He was all over—ah…" She tried to calm down. "He was attentive, interested, he couldn't look at me enough like I'm really something."

"Becca Salt, you damn well better listen to me." Rowena had never used such a harsh tone or expletives when speaking to her. "You are something. You're everything that's right with this world. How many times do I have to tell you that?"

"You're my mother. Of course, you think I'm wonderful. If I were Medusa, you'd find something good to say about me. It's him I'm worried about."

"Why? Sounds as though he's seriously into you."

Becca jumped from her chair and strode across the room. "You didn't answer me." She ached with tension and uncertainty. "Did you put anything in the second potion to make him think I'm pretty, sexy, hot, whatever you want to call it?"

"Of course not. Why would I? You're all those things already. He'd have to be blind not to see it."

Becca rolled her eyes and stopped pacing. "You're sure? I'm not accusing you or anything, but maybe you did it by accident?"

"I know how to make a potion. If you'd studied a little harder and respected magic, you would, too."

That again. Becca gritted her teeth and spoke through them. "What did you have the second potion do? What were you expecting?"

"Exactly what you wanted. To turn him back to the way he was before you gave him the first potion."

"Nothing else?"

"You didn't ask for anything else."

Then it was true. Eric liked her because he actually did. How was that possible? Stuff like this never happened to her. She could handle all the shit the world shoveled out, but she wasn't prepared for happiness. Dizzy, she could barely stand and sank to the sofa, ready to cry in relief and joy. Before she could, an awful thought struck. "That doesn't make sense."

"Why not?"

"When I gave him the second potion, he went back to looking like the regular Eric, but he definitely didn't act that way."

"What do you mean?"

He had commanded her to go to him and they'd kissed. He'd ordered her to strip. She had. Triple-X rated activities followed. She gave her mother the G-rated version. "He acted like he was interested in me. Really interested."

"And you're convinced the second potion was responsible?"

"Either that or how it interacted with the first one. What else could explain it? The man was on fire. He wanted to be sexy, commanding, all that bad boy stuff, and he was. Your potion, or potions, did that."

"They. Did. Not," Rowena muttered beneath her breath. "They don't interact with each other. One simply cancels the other out, which is what you asked me to do. To get him back to the way he'd been. Frankly, I'm glad I did, considering his language. Just awful. He shouldn't talk around you like that."

"Mom, please, can we stay on the subject?"

She huffed. "Very well. Are you ready to listen? More importantly, are you prepared to believe?"

This sounded like Mulder lecturing Scully about paranormal activities in the *X-Files*. "Depends. If this is fact-based, I'm on board. If it's simply a feeling you have then I might need convincing."

"You are the fact and you'd see that if you weren't so down on yourself. Honestly, I did not raise you to be that way."

"I know and I'm sorry. All I can say is going through puberty and adolescence was no picnic."

"It wasn't for me, either. It isn't for anyone. However, the rest of us have moved on. You need to, also. You're the one who brought out that other aspect of Eric's personality. Not that I approve."

"That's impossible. The potions had to have done this."

"Becca, I'm your mother. I wouldn't give any man anything to make him behave that way around my daughter. I want you to be with a nice guy. Not some jerk who treats you badly."

Never had Becca been as confused. "He didn't. He was simply more confident than he's been in the past, according to him. But that doesn't make sense."

"Why?"

"He's dated thousands of women. All of them gorgeous, I'm sure. Oh, hey, wait, that's probably it. I'm not gorgeous, so he could be however he wanted with me. Why didn't I see that before?" She smacked her forehead. "That explains a lot."

"It doesn't explain anything, unless he did treat you badly."

"I swear he didn't. He couldn't have been nicer, yet assertive…in a good way."

"And that doesn't tell you anything?"

"Like what? He's beyond hot?"

Rowena sighed loudly. "Maybe he's finally met the woman he's been looking for all along. The kind he needs. The one who lets him be who he really is."

Becca rested her hand on her chest. Her heart whapped away, trying to break through her ribs. "You mean me?"

"Who else? Sounds as though he really likes you. The way mortals do. When it comes to love, humans have it all over witches, warlocks, gods and what-have-you. They take risks we're too afraid to even think about. We rely on magic or powers. They expose themselves, right down to their souls."

Tears filled Becca's eyes. "Mom, do you really think he feels that way about me?"

"He'd be crazy not to. But, speaking as one woman to another, not as a mother to her daughter, I'd say it definitely sounds like he wants you."

Becca moaned.

"Baby, that's a good thing."

"What if I waited too long? He's called several times. I've been dodging him. I didn't want to get hurt. What if he's given up?"

"Then he's not the man for you. Oh, baby." Rowena spoke more gently. "Your father would have braved everyone in my coven to make me his. And, trust me, they're not beings to mess with. Isn't Eric like that?"

"I don't know."

"Then you better find out. Oh, and Becca?"

"Yeah?"

"There is one sure way to tell if magic, not you, changed him."

"How?"

As Rowena explained, a smile filled her voice.

Chapter Eleven

Sprawled on his sofa, Eric clicked the TV remote repeatedly. Sports channels zipped by. Tonight's games didn't appeal to him.

He tried the adult channels next. They were as bad, failing to hold his attention for more than a few seconds. He pointed the remote, stilled and leaned over to follow the actors' sexual contortions, their torsos and limbs twisted in unnatural positions.

Maybe this wouldn't be too bad.

He got up to speed on the scant plot quickly. One performer played a schoolteacher, the other a principal. The teacher, a guy who looked dumb enough to have failed kindergarten, bent backwards over his desk. The principal, a young woman who didn't seem old enough to have graduated high school, crawled all over him, her skirt hiked up to expose her lacy white thong.

The camera zoomed in on her perfectly shaped ass then rose to her pinned-up hair. It came loose on its own. Her dark brown curls tumbled to his bare chest.

They went at each other, moaning and panting, scattering the teacher's pencils, papers and books, which made an enormous racket.

Like that wouldn't bring in the school board to get them both fired. Eric muttered an oath and searched for a true-to-life storyline on the other adult channels. Something with a financial analyst and a half-witch.

He came up with zip and returned to the first film. Apparently, his profession was so damn dull even mortal women wouldn't frolic naked in a financial advisor's office.

He ached to call Becca. Again. Four times, he'd left her messages. Four times, she hadn't phoned back. Twice, he'd driven by her office to corner her there, but ditched those plans fast. He had some pride left. Granted, not a lot, but he wasn't going to grovel. At least not tonight. Maybe next week.

Growls and squeals poured from the TV. A pizza delivery guy had joined the principal and teacher's carnal action for a no-holds-barred ménage. Books and notepads flew.

Whoever wrote this damn thing didn't know realistic from deep-down stupid. Eric frowned at the time. A freaking hour had passed and his pizza still wasn't here.

He should have ordered from Domino's or Little Caesars. But, no, he'd called Desiderio's because Desi had always insisted Eric come to him for his pies. That way they'd get cooked right and delivered when promised.

Eric couldn't recall when his uncle had guaranteed delivery for the damn food. His belly growled. He grabbed his phone. His doorbell ding-dong-dinged.

About fucking time.

He was going to give the delivery guy hell and not tip him more than three dollars. Maybe four. Okay, five. The poor slob had to make a living. Besides, it wasn't his fault the pizza was so damn late. Desi had done this on purpose, still pissed because Eric had dared ask if he'd messed with Becca's food and his.

Desi had kept yelling that he should have but hadn't.

Eric wished he had. He could try the teacher's moves on Becca.

The teacher was naked as the day he'd been born and tore at the principal's slutty-prim clothing. She scratched his pecs with her blood-red nails. The pizza guy dropped pepperoni on her waxed cunt and ate it off as the teacher dipped his cock between her willing lips.

The football captain rushed inside and blurted an apology about being late for his remedial math appointment.

The others moaned and writhed.

Mr. Football dropped his calculus book. He tore off his school jacket, tee and jeans and joined the fray.

The doorbell rang again.

With his attention riveted to the porn, Eric padded to the damn door and swung it open. "Here." Blindly, he shoved bills in the guy's general direction.

The dude ran his fingers down Eric's arm to his chest.

Eric dropped the bills and jerked away, ready to slug...Becca?

Her hand was a breath away from his fly. She gripped the handle on a large wicker basket that held gingham napkins, a bottle of Desi's most expensive wine and a boxed pizza from his place.

He reeled.

She was actually here, ready to see and feed him in more ways than one?

She'd dressed for it. Her top tied beneath her breasts, the neckline cut low enough to accentuate her sensational cleavage. It and her harem pants were a lustrous silver fabric that brought out the blue in her eyes. She wore toe rings, delicate chains around one ankle and her starry navel jewelry. Those baubles rolled across her sweet belly with each breath.

She took quite a few, the same as him. At this rate, they'd use up the available oxygen.

Eric opened his mouth to say something, anything but nothing came out.

Mr. Football's loud, pleased grunt blasted from the TV.

Becca leaned to the side to see past his arm. "He sounds happy."

He did. Eric wasn't feeling so great even though she was only inches from him. At last.

He'd called her four damn times with no response. He'd tried to talk to her in his car. She'd fled. She'd made herself scarce. She'd made him want. And now that she was ready to move forward with their relationship, if that's what this was about, she expected him to greet her with open arms?

Eric crossed his.

The principal whimpered then let out a lusty moan.

Becca's cheeks colored slightly but still looked pale in contrast to the black stuff around her eyes and her maroon lipstick. Makeup she'd worn the first time he'd seen her when she'd ordered him to get naked and he'd obeyed without question.

Remembering, Eric tightened his arms and kept on his clothes. No more Mr. Nice Guy for him.

She shifted her weight. "Hi."

Her breathy voice turned his legs to rubber. His cock went to full alert. Ready to roll.

He wouldn't allow that. This wasn't some dumb adult film where she could waltz back into his life, cover him with pepperoni and lick it off. What they'd shared had been real magic, and she'd refused to believe it. Time to give her a taste of her own medicine. "Clearly, you need a financial analyst."

Her reddish eyebrows lifted at his comment or coolish tone. She chose to ignore his pissy mood and offered an unhurried smile that went beyond suggestive, straight into wanton. "That's why I'm here. For you. A financial analyst."

She trailed her finger over his crossed arms and down his tee to his jeans waistband.

His heart broke a little more, wounded by her past actions. His cock, on the other hand, responded like a lovesick puppy ready to forgive, and tried to wiggle past his fly to her hand.

Before she noticed and knew how much he'd missed her, Eric stepped back. "That's not what I mean. If you're delivering pizza for Desi now, your business is obviously in trouble."

Uncertainty replaced her kittenish come-on. She ditched her smile. "The service is doing fine. Great, in fact. Customers round the clock."

"So you said the last time we were together. Yet, you're here, not there. Why? Isn't this your busy time? All those vamps hiding from the sun and the weres looking for a full moon?"

Blood drained from her face. She glanced down the hall.

He guessed to see if his neighbors were around and had heard what he'd said.

They weren't and hadn't.

She sighed. "I know you're pissed and you have every right to be." She lifted her face to his. "I'm so sorry. Can we talk inside? Please?"

The pizza delivery guy groaned. "More, dammit more."

Becca's blush stained her throat and chest. Her breasts lifted and fell with her anxious breathing. Her soft globes quivered slightly.

His shaft thickened beyond what he'd believed possible. Not trusting his voice, he stepped aside to let her pass.

She gaped at his one-hundred-and-ten-inch TV screen. "Wow, that's big."

The teacher's cock looked like an anaconda even from where Eric stood. He slammed the door.

Becca flinched but didn't look at him.

He wasn't surprised. She was still running away, preferring to glance at his living room, its vanilla-white walls, the glass-and-chrome furniture. Nothing quirky like her treatment room décor, or possibly her apartment that she'd refused to let him see.

She put her basket on his coffee table. The metal base was pure *Star Trek*, circles within circles similar to Saturn's rings. His leather sectional was large enough for four couples to screw on comfortably.

The actors were really going at it now.

Becca watched for a second then turned to him, pouty lips parted, nipples erect, her features yearning.

Eric had to lock his knees to keep from rushing closer and gathering her in his arms. They couldn't simply jump each other as though nothing had happened. So much had changed. After dating too many women who'd treated him as a diversion until someone better came along, he'd found Becca. One in a bajillion. He'd opened up to her as he'd never done with another woman. And she fucking ran away.

This last week had been the worst in his life, and Eric wanted her to know he wasn't playing at his feelings for her or their relationship. With Becca, there would be no games. "You said you wanted to talk. About what?"

She fingered her silver stars, either nervous or trying to turn him on.

He was far beyond that, straight into raw desire.

"Us?" She looked at him expectantly.

"You're not sure? Still?"

"Oh, yeah. That is, I want to talk about you and me. Together. As a couple." She bit her lip. "You know."

He had since their night at Desiderio's. "Why? All of a sudden?" He padded closer. "I called you four times. You never answered or got back to me. You did get my voicemails, right?"

"Uh-huh."

"You don't seem certain."

"I am." She nodded so vigorously her hair fell past her ear and skimmed her cheek.

Eric wanted to ease it away, kiss her senseless and welcome her back into his life. He forced himself to stay put. "Then you knew days ago that I wanted to talk, but you didn't bother to return my calls."

"I was scared."

"And I wasn't?"

She rounded the table.

He stepped back.

She halted. "I didn't think about that."

"Obviously." He frowned. "So, you think I'm made of stone?"

"No, of course not. It's just that no one's ever wanted me before. Not like you did. I couldn't believe that you really felt that way on your own."

Eric wasn't certain what pissed him off more — Becca not seeing how hot she was, that she hadn't had enough confidence in his feelings to trust her own or that she finally had proof of what he felt and had relied on that, rather than her intolerable need, to come here.

He gestured to her basket. "I take it you've talked to Desi about screwing around with our food."

"He didn't."

"Yeah, I know."

She didn't look surprised. "He told me you talked to him, too."

Eric's outrage fell away, replaced by embarrassment. He'd also had his doubts, which he'd tried to talk out with her. He hadn't fled.

Becca took a halting step in his direction.

Eric stayed where he was.

Relief flooded her features.

He was about to explode. Too many emotions raged through him. Wonder, lust, hurt and tenderness.

"I called my mom." She smiled briefly. "Her second potion turned you back to the way you were when you initially came to my place. It neutralized the first potion completely without adding any additional magic."

"Yeah, I know."

Shock registered in her eyes. "You talked to her?"

"I didn't have to. Deep down, I knew you, and only you, had caused the change in me."

"Deep down?"

"Yeah. My heart, soul and guts."

Her mood changed from hesitant to knowing. "So, even after talking with your uncle, you had to think about what happened between us and dig deeper, because you weren't totally certain, either."

"Of you? How could I be? But I was willing to discuss whatever problems we had. You weren't."

Her eyes got shiny. "I shouldn't have run."

If one tear fell, he was going to die. "No, you shouldn't have."

"Can we talk now? Is it too late?"

"We've been talking."

Her mouth turned down. "You can't forgive me?"

"Did I say that?"

"No. But you're still pissed."

His emotions went way deeper than anything he sensed she could imagine or accept. "Let's just say this isn't getting us anywhere."

Panic tore across her face. She snatched in a tiny breath.

Eric warned himself not to react as he wanted — excusing what had happened, saying it didn't matter, behaving like a nice guy rather than a man she'd torn to shreds with her absence and silence.

Resolved, he told her the score. "I don't want to go through another minute of the hell you've put us through because you don't trust yourself, me or whatever. Be mine, dammit, and fight for what we have or else let's forget it."

Becca stopped flapping her hand to stave off tears. Her eyes brimmed with them. "I don't want to forget it."

His spirits skyrocketed. He corralled them to take this slow. Or at least at a less than supersonic pace. "Neither do I."

However, he had to prove to Becca that he wanted her for who she was. How she talked, behaved and looked. The biggest hurdle yet. He leaned down until their noses nearly touched. "My teeth are hurting I want you so badly, and that includes physically. I'm not going to apologize for thinking you're fucking gorgeous."

Her skin got rosier than in the past. Surprise and joy lit her face. "I wouldn't expect you to."

"Prove it. Strip for me."

"What?"

"Take off your clothes. Prove you believe what I've said about how awesome you are." He gave her only enough space to pull off her duds.

Becca eyed his clothes. "You're going to stay dressed while I strip?"

"That's right."

The principal gasped in the movie.

Becca glanced at the action.

"Uh-uh." Eric eased her face back to his. "Look at me while you strip. Unless you don't want to do this."

Her reddened cheeks matched her hair color. "I do." She toed off her right sandal.

"Nope. Put it back on. The heels and jewelry stay. Everything else goes. Slowly. You rush, and we'll start over until you get it right."

Her brows drew together.

Eric stared her down, confident in what she wanted. Him and only him.

Dutifully and without rushing, Becca undid her top. The lightweight fabric fell away to reveal her lacy black bra. It had the same half cups she'd worn earlier that revealed her nipples. Rosy. Tight. Perfect for his mouth.

A delighted growl stuck in his throat.

He inched closer and caught her scent. Witchy with a hint of pepperoni from the pizza she'd put in her basket. His mouth watered but not for the food. "Undo the bra."

She stroked the front clasp.

Mesmerized didn't begin to describe the effect that had on him.

She twisted the clasp back and forth. The two halves parted. The cups pulled away from each other and exposed her breasts slowly. As he'd demanded.

Eric wasn't certain he wanted that any longer. The promise of caressing and licking her nipples and his cock being deep inside her cunt was a powerful motivator to rip off her clothes.

He resisted. He'd waited a damn week for her. No, he'd waited his entire adult life and wasn't going to race through this. They'd done that in the treatment room and at the restaurant. Tonight, he was going to prolong every damn minute they made love. Already, they'd gone past fucking to something deep and lasting.

He hoped.

Her cups pulled away completely.

His mouth went dry. Her nipples' delicate pink tint brought to mind spring, soft breezes and not-so-gentle nights wrapped in her eager caress.

She pulled off her top and bra. The garments fell to the floor.

The football captain gushed from the screen. "Awesome."

He had no idea. Becca's breasts were more than a handful, perfect for Eric. "Put your arms behind your back. No, wait. Lift them above your head."

Becca worried her bottom lip.

He figured she was anxious about her appearance. "I'll help." He rested her arms over her head and stepped back.

His legs almost gave out, that was how scrumptious she was. Pale skin wrapped in softness and heat. He padded from side to side, spellbound by her supple globes, tight areolas and long tips. A mole graced her waist. A smaller one adorned her torso. A faint blue vein followed the curve on her breast.

His jeans felt too snug. Thankfully, he hadn't worn underwear that would have further trapped his monster erection. "Go on. Strip."

She regarded her boobs then him. "I'll have to lower my arms."

"Just don't cross them in front and hide yourself from me."

Her face turned crimson. She plucked her waistband. The elastic rode her hips like Eric wanted to, their groins kissing, his rod nestled deep, his balls swinging toward her.

Becca made a noise that was part wounded kitten, part she-devil.

He hoped her desire would win. To him, this wasn't only about passion. He wanted her to know how beautiful she was and to believe it as much as he did.

She eased her pants to her knees. They floated to the gleaming hardwood floor. She hooked her thumbs beneath her underwear.

"Wait." Like her bra, her thong was black and lacy but so sheer her reddish curls were visible. Embroidered roses decorated the fabric. Men survived brutal wars in order to return home to stuff like this.

He stroked the dainty flowers and the lace-edged waistband.

Becca arched her back, which pushed her breasts at him.

Eric sweated. The room whirled. With tremendous willpower, he ignored her succulent offering and stepped back. "Off. I want you nude."

She pressed her hand to her throat. "Give me a sec to calm down. I can barely breathe."

"You can breathe later. Do what I said." He would have added please, but couldn't pull in enough air to beg.

Her eyes glittered and her complexion glowed. She eased the thong to her upper thighs, revealing her curls.

Moisture glistened on her thatch and crotch. She was drenched for him, willing and wanting.

A magical moment.

Becca pushed the underwear to her ankles.

Eric offered his hand, grateful it didn't shake.

Becca squeezed his fingers and stepped away from her clothes. She looked better than any babe in an adult film, or those who'd populated his teenage wet dreams. The only thing she wore was her blush, makeup, funky jewelry and heels.

The pizza guy bellowed in the movie. "Oh, yeah!"

Eric wrapped his arm around her waist. "Come on."

He led her into his bedroom and flicked on the lights.

Becca blinked. Intense illumination poured from chrome table lamps and ceiling fixtures. One shone on his king-size bed, its mattress draped in a black-and-silver comforter. The furniture faced a mirrored wall separated into three sections. Each sported a crystal knob. In a Dom's fantasy, they would have opened onto an area storing chains, whips and riding crops.

Becca guessed Eric had once kept his baggy boxers inside. Now, he was into stretchy, revealing underwear and was very sure of himself, because of her. Holy crap, what had she unleashed?

Time to find out. Not only was she hornier than hell and hopelessly in love — once they were doing the nasty he couldn't dwell on her imperfect nudity. She rushed to the bed.

He stopped her. "Lots of closet space in here." He pulled her to the mirrors and turned her to face them. "That's why I got this place." Positioned behind her, he rested his hands on her shoulders. His fingers dipped close to her nipples.

Those babies puckered up so much they ached. Becca sagged against him. "What are we doing way over here when the bed's that way?" She jabbed her thumb at it.

"Look at yourself in the mirror."

She couldn't. Wouldn't.

"Uh-uh." He settled his mouth on her ear. "Open your eyes. Watch what I do to you."

Even her belly button burned from her blush. "Ah…"

"No arguments." He ground his hips into her ass, his cock as hard as his words. "You're going to do what I say, Becca. Beginning now."

Eric snuggled his tongue in her ear.

She trembled.

He bit her lobe playfully and gave her an openmouthed kiss on her neck. "If you don't, this isn't happening."

"What?"

"You heard me."

That she had, but didn't believe a word he'd said. No way could he stop now, any more than she could. She spoke to his reflection. "You'd really tell me to leave?"

"I'd let you go." He cupped her breasts and dragged his thumbs over her nipples.

Pleasure arrowed straight to her pussy.

"I'm not playing anymore, Becca. Neither are you." He fondled her gently and breathed nearly as hard as she did. "You're fucking gorgeous, and you're going to start looking at yourself as everyone else sees you."

What he proposed was impossible. She was plain and plump, not even close to pretty. Not like her mom, Heather or Constance. They were exquisite. She was barely ordinary.

"Look at yourself." He stroked her collarbone. "Such luscious skin, not a flaw on it. Your long legs. Curves that don't quit. That red hair." He pressed his cheek to hers. "The stuff on your head is nice, too."

Becca laughed.

"And your eyes...wow." Wonder welled in his gaze, similar to someone having a religious experience. "They're pure blue. Like Windex."

She giggled and smacked his arm.

"You don't believe me?" Using his body, he pushed her closer to the mirror. "You tell me what you see."

A woman ignored by men so easily. She'd wanted to be accepted and popular like the others in her class, but wasn't, so she became an outcast who'd dressed unconventionally and acted any damn way she chose to prove she didn't care, when she did. *Far too much.*

Gently, Eric cradled her breasts. "What do you see, Becca?"

Your acceptance and something akin to worship. Maybe the beginning of love. "What I've needed for too long."

He smiled. "That's a good start. Now, watch." He dipped one hand to the curls between her legs, separated her folds and stroked her cleft.

Every nerve ending she owned came alive beneath his fingertips. She bloomed with his passionate attention. The doubt she'd shouldered for too many years drained away, along with her heartache.

To Becca's amazement, she looked wanton and sexy. Definitely fine. "You put a spell on me."

"Nope. Just giving you some foreplay. I've had a lot of practice."

With thousands of women. Maybe millions. Becca elbowed him.

He grunted loudly.

A put on. She'd barely touched him. "That's not what I meant. Look at me."

"I haven't stopped."

"I'm…" She didn't finish. Couldn't.

"What?"

Her coloring and features had come together in a way Becca had never seen or noticed before. Not as Eric had. She looked at herself through his eyes, appreciating her stunning red hair, deep blue eyes, milky skin and striking features. "You sure you haven't used magic on me?"

"I don't use spells. I use arrows, or I'm supposed to."

"You must have nailed me with one when I wasn't paying attention. I look good."

"Oh, hell, you look way better than that."

He rubbed her clit hard and fast.

Her mouth sagged open. She pushed to her toes and dropped back down. Her anklets jiggled and her stars bobbed north and south. She squirmed against Eric, wanting him to continue but also needing him to stop.

The mounting tension was more than she could endure. Color rose in her cheeks and throat. She was practically dripping between her legs.

Eric used her moisture to arouse her further.

The climax slashed through her so quickly she let out a wild cry unlike any she'd made in her life. Incomparable delight welled, receded and returned to touch her everywhere. She couldn't stop trembling. If not for Eric supporting her, she would have dropped to the floor.

He swept her into his arms as he would a woman who weighed nothing. Definitely not her, but she appreciated the gesture and cuddled close, her head on his shoulder. She drew his initials and hers on his tee and surrounded them with a heart. Silly, she knew but didn't care, because it was also precious.

Eric yanked down the comforter and lowered her to the mattress. The linens smelled as clean as he did.

He leaned over her. "What did you just see?"

My wish come true. "Heaven."

His grin couldn't have been wider. He pulled off his tee and jeans. Spectacularly nude, he followed his cock, which pointed straight at her. His balls were already snug against his body, possibly ready to release their load.

Becca held out her arms to him and parted her legs with more confidence than she'd done with any man. For Eric, she was enough, beautiful just as she was. The greatest compliment any man could give a woman. "Climb on, baby. I'm going to give you the ride of your life."

He prowled toward her. "Not so fast." His voice was gritty. "My place, my rules."

"Aw, shit, we're going back to the mirrors?"

His shoulders shook with his suppressed laughter. He sobered quickly. "Go to your hands and knees and face your reflection."

Although reluctant, Becca obeyed. Her breasts hung like overripe fruit, ready for him to pluck and taste. The thought dampened her cunt.

He climbed on the bed. The mattress shook from his weight. He settled between her legs and ran his crown down her slit. His satisfied grin turned downright goofy.

His joy aroused and touched Becca in more ways than she could have imagined.

He stared at her ass or his cock or both. "Are you watching yourself?"

"Yeah." A lie. She had eyes only for him.

He beamed and drove inside her, his chin lifted to the ceiling, the veins in his neck distended enough to burst.

Becca sucked air at his rigidity and size. He was bigger than the last time they'd slept together. Not from the potion. Her.

What a miracle their meeting had turned out to be. She gripped the bedspread, lifted her ass and gave him full reign over her pride and heart. He'd treat both well.

He rode her slowly.

She'd never experienced anything so breathtaking and tightened her cunt around his shaft.

His pecs danced with each thrust. His already firm belly grew tauter.

The man was definitely gorgeous and hung. A true god.

The friction between their bodies built to a dangerous level.

Eric gripped her hips and pumped wildly.

She gasped in pleasure.

His hair jumped over his forehead. His complexion darkened to a dusky red. If he clenched his teeth any harder, he'd grind them to dust.

Becca was in danger of doing the same thing. Each pump drove her closer to ecstasy.

Surely, he couldn't take much more.

He rubbed her clit.

Someone shouted. Could have been her. Too much pleasure stormed through Becca. Control wasn't possible. In another sec, she'd behave worse than her clients or the actress in Eric's X-rated flick.

He growled, groaned and grunted. The sounds she loved most.

On a reckless bellow, he came and drove her over the edge a second time. Her endurance at an end.

Damp and shaky, he kissed her spine. His gasps warmed her.

Becca labored to speak. A wheeze came out.

Eric panted. "What?"

"Rest." She patted the mattress.

He made a disdainful sound. "You think I can't keep going?"

If not, he'd die trying. Exactly like a mortal guy. "You're a god, not Super Dick."

Eric laughed and pulled Becca to her knees, his cock still inside her sheath.

"What are you doing?"

Using one hand, he held hers to her chest. With his other, he lightly stroked her clit. "What do you think?"

She couldn't answer. He made her burn for everything he could give. Fully imprisoned by him, she yielded. Their hearts beat as one. The mirrors showed their indecent pose that was also wonderful and accentuated their differences. His hard, masculine form. Her soft curves.

What little strength Becca had weakened further with his strokes. She peaked again from his talented touch, and more importantly, from the way he regarded her. With male lust and an emotional tenderness that rocked her world.

They collapsed to the bed where Eric took her repeatedly.

After a brief rest, she strutted around his apartment in the nude, something she never would have done with another guy. They ate bare-assed and watched porn flicks, comparing the actors' moves to their own.

Theirs were always better.

When interesting positions came up, they put the TV on slow-mo and mimicked the moves. She pulled a muscle in her neck. He strained one in his back. They massaged each other to good health and carried on.

A long time later, they lay on the bed, limbs entwined, mouths joined, tongues still waltzing. Sated from the best sex ever, Becca welcomed this intimacy, loving how Eric tasted and smelled. A lot like him, a little like her. They'd marked each other.

Their kisses were sloppy and joyous, romantic and searching.

Eventually, they quieted down and simply gazed at each other. Although they were beat, neither would succumb to sleep.

He smiled first and touched her nose. "What do you see, Becca?"

An end to loneliness. A future with him at my side. "What I can't live without."

He traced her mouth and ruffled her lashes.

She giggled.

"So, you believe me now. That what happened tonight came from the real me and because of you, nothing else."

"A little bit was due to the flicks we watched."

"Those were my new moves, not what's in my heart."

Becca pushed to one elbow and smoothed back his hair. "Yeah, I know. And I do believe you."

"You're absolutely certain?"

She'd known from the way he'd kissed, caressed and made love to her that he'd behaved that way from something deep inside. A power she'd unleashed in him, making him part bad boy, mostly nice guy, totally her guy.

However, she also recalled what her mom said about one indisputable sign. Becca had been too distracted by their good time to look for it, though she would now. She leaned up. The mirror reflected his ass.

Rowena had said any potion that altered the way Eric usually behaved would also change another part on him.

A perfect Cupid's heart still graced his right butt cheek.

Becca's heart soared at the final proof that the potions hadn't done anything to him.

She alone had and intended to keep things that way.

Epilogue

Several months later…

Red balloons emblazoned with *Congratulations!* in huge silver letters decorated the private meeting room at Desiderio's. An enormous scarlet banner with the same word ran across one wall. Flowers abounded. The buffet boasted Italian antipasti, spinach and artichoke dip, tiny meatballs, more salads than a vegan could eat in a month, chicken marsala and piccata, lasagna, eggplant parmesan and baked ziti. Tiramisu, cannoli, zeppole, tartufo and panettone rounded out dessert. The open bar served every liquor known to man.

There was even a band playing popular tunes. Thankfully, the opera stuff with the shrieking soprano didn't bleed into this space.

Becca leaned into Eric. "Was Desi aware this gathering was for a work-related thing not a wedding or a wake?"

"I told him that but he never listens. He insisted that your service reaching its thousandth customer was a huge deal. On that, I have to agree." He brushed his lips over hers. "You're amazing."

In his eyes, she was, and that was all that mattered. For Becca, she was at peace with herself, thanks to his love. It gave her the courage to be stupid at times and to make mistakes. When they argued, she knew they'd eventually cool off and would return to each other, ready to try again. Just like her mom and dad always did. She and Eric weathered crazy work schedules, being paranormals and simply living. They grew their friendship and ran heedlessly into love.

She was so happy, she wanted the same for her BFFs. Tonight, hadn't really been about her business success, but an excuse to introduce Constance, Heather and Zoe to some nice guys so they'd have a chance to have what she did.

Unfortunately, Becca didn't know a lot of decent dudes. The males she came into contact with were customers at the service. With their problems not yet solved, she didn't want to inflict them on anyone. That left men Eric knew.

He'd invited his many cousins to the party. All handsome as hell and so preppy they could have populated a Brooks Brothers' ad. At last count, the ratio of males to females in here was seven to one.

Good odds.

A blond twentysomething with close-cropped hair stood next to Zoe at the buffet. His smile was so perfect it looked painted on. "I understand what you're saying about suffering, and I get how that can build character. To a point. If the agony is unending, though, why go on? Most people would check out at that point and I can't blame them. I think it's better to cut folks a little slack, especially if you can use white, not dark, power to make things better."

Zoe's hair and shoulders smoked. "Maybe for you, but not for me." Her eyes flamed. "What you said is doing things the sissy way."

He traded a pained glance with Eric and took off for a table in the far corner.

Eric inclined his head to another cousin. The guy slumped but dutifully dragged up to Zoe to engage her in what would probably be a brutal conversation about good and evil. He and the other one breathed through their mouths to avoid her sulfur stench.

Becca pressed her lips to Eric's ear. "How much did you pay them and your other cousins to be here tonight?"

"Nothing. I'm working on their 401ks and retirement plans for nothing."

She patted his firm belly. "You're a good man. At least Constance is having a great time."

Numerous cousins were lined up behind her, doing the conga to Maroon 5's 'Moves Like Jagger'. The tune and footwork didn't match, but their laughter said they didn't care. Becca hoped at least one would connect with her. If not, she'd try something else. She'd found her guy and by God, Constance would too.

As far as Heather was concerned…

She stood two feet away from a cousin Eric had introduced her to then told them to dance. The young man in question was cute, his hair black, eyes green. He looked at her shyly. She blushed bright red and averted her gaze. They bobbed in time to the music, no foot or hand movements, no shaking their booties.

Eric rubbed his mouth.

Becca elbowed him. "Are you laughing?"

He turned around and hung his head. "No." His shoulders shook.

She tried to explain. "Heather's a good fairy. She's like really pure."

"Maybe you should pour some liquor into her. Get her to relax."

That would probably give her PTSD. "She's never been around men romantically. Once she loosens up with your cousin, she can move on to a guy who actually talks."

"Hey, Tommy's a good kid. Maybe you should cast a spell on him and her so they can get it on. You have said you've been practicing."

Not that much. Even her mom would have trouble with them. "Tell you what, you go first and shoot your special arrows. I'll wait. I'll watch. I'll even pray."

Laughing, he slung his arm around her shoulder and shook her. "No fucking chance. Let's say we let nature take its course with your buddies, especially Heather. Let them find love the way we did."

"We just stumbled upon it."

"And groped our way through, the blind leading the clueless. I'm the clueless one, by the way. Yet everything still worked out."

"With a lot of luck."

"Uh-uh. With something else." He gathered her close and kissed her hard. "Endless attraction, complete trust and everlasting loyalty."

The best kind of magic.

Enchanted and bewitched by her guy, Becca forgot everyone else. Music and colors faded, conversations floated away, only he remained.

Bound to each other through good and bad, they swayed to a slow dance of their own making, their smiles meant for each other.

Their hearts and souls one.

Want to see more from this author?
Here's a taster for you to enjoy!

Taming the Beast:
Surrendering to the Beast
Tina Donahue

Excerpt

Heather clasped her hands to her chest, lowered her head and tried to believe as she never had before. "You can do this, you can do this, you *can* do this."

Her personal mantra, gained from countless self-improvement books, online courses and seminars she'd attended. The writers and sponsors always promised the programs would make her a new woman in business, life and love.

As a good fairy, that wasn't likely, but she needed all the help she could get. Born to be kind, patient, sympathetic to a fault and purer than the driven snow, she simply wasn't assertive enough during work hours or on the dating scene. Not that she'd ever tried to hook up with guys. Even thinking about talking to one in a romantic sense made her dizzy enough to pass out. Since none had flocked to her on their own, especially the shy ones who'd prove non-threatening, she was lonely and wanting.

That left her career to fill the endless hours where her innate personality still got in the way. Always, she feared hurting someone's feelings no matter the consequences to herself, her BFFs or the business where she and they worked.

Serving as the receptionist and healer at From Crud to Stud, a New Orleans makeover service for supernatural beings, was a monumental undertaking. She had an honor-bound duty to make certain the clients left there healthy and hearty, that their appointments were up-to-date and that they never stiffed the service on money they owed. Being an overdue bill collector was the hardest part of her job description.

But it had to be done. Right now. She'd delayed too long on this account and only had herself to blame.

Nausea rolled through her as she steeled herself to do battle with Satan. To her horror, her Skype call to him connected instantly. Her vision dimmed but she faced her webcam and his image on her computer monitor.

This evening, he resembled a European playboy, a cognac snifter in one hand. He'd slicked back his dark hair and wore a blood-red ascot that contrasted nicely with his white shirt and navy blazer.

For a bad guy, he certainly knew how to dress.

"*Cara mia.*" Heat smoldered in his voice and dark eyes. "What can I do to you?"

She wanted to hurl but gave him her sternest look. "I'm sorry, I don't mean to correct you, but I think you meant *for* me not *to* me." He never got the phrase right.

Grinning, he focused on her white peasant blouse and jutted nipples, her areolas tightened from the chilly weather, not him. Tonight was damp and cool, thanks to a spring storm that raged in the French Quarter. Lightning flashed. The office lights flickered. Just like in a slasher film.

Flames flared briefly in his pupils.

They didn't calm her apprehension.

He leaned closer to the screen, his eyes boring into her. "We'll do many things to each other, no?"

Heather would have given anything to flee but pretended she hadn't heard his vulgar question. A knee-jerk reaction for someone with her genetic makeup. Needing to get tough, she held up his overdue bill and hoped he'd look at it rather than her chest. Her hand shook so badly the paper rattled.

"How you tremble," he cooed. "How pale you are. Allow me to put some color in your lovely cheeks. Heat that will last an eternity."

Her skin grew clammy. "Please, just pay your account." She waved the paper and prayed she wouldn't lose her nerve. "Your grandson failed to show for his last two appointments. I'm sure he had a good reason. Unfortunately, he didn't call to cancel. Because you're the cardholder, we had to charge you for the time. I'm so sorry, really I am, but it is the rule."

One she was obligated to enforce to keep this place solvent and humming. In the treatment rooms, vampires hissed, weres howled and demons snarled obscenities. She cringed at that awful language but understood their pain and the others' agony, too. These poor souls suffered proverbial hell to suppress their beasts so they could date mortal women without freaking them out, while also winning their hearts the normal way. With real charm, not magic. With integrity and love, not lies and manipulation.

Those miracle transformations didn't come easily or cheap. They took the staff's valuable time and clients needed to pay for the effort. Even Satan should understand such a simple and fair concept.

He offered an indulgent look. "What charges?"

His bill burst into flames.

Heather gasped and dropped the paper in her trashcan.

"Later." He killed the call.

She smothered the small blaze and chided herself for not having been firm with Satan's grandson when he'd signed up for the service. Determined to make up for being too nice, she brought up her bank account to pay the charges herself. After that, she'd book a spot at another assertiveness training workshop. One had to do the trick for her. Clinging to that hope, she filled in the required spaces on her online payment form.

The lights flickered twice, thunder boomed and the front door flew open.

It banged against the wall.

She flinched.

Dank air and rain blew inside, followed by a guy who looked to be thirty or so. He wore a black cowboy hat, snug navy tee, low-slung jeans and cowboy boots.

He shoved the door shut, slumped against it and breathed hard.

Heather shot to her feet. Her chair rolled into the numerous potted plants behind her.

He didn't notice. His eyes were closed, face raised to the ceiling. His prominent Adam's apple bobbed from his hard swallow.

Although alarmed at his entrance and who he might be, she was also intrigued. Something that had never happened before when it came to a guy who might not be a customer here. On those occasions, she'd always hurried in the opposite direction.

Her legs refused to move.

Short, dark hairs dusted his throat. Rain dampened his cocoa-colored hair. Those thick, wavy tresses flowed to his broad shoulders that heaved with his ragged breaths. Tall, six-three or so, he was nicely muscular.

Virility she found protective rather than daunting.

His wet tee clung to his well-defined pecs and abs, those bruising biceps. His bronze skin betrayed an outdoorsy nature rather than a guy who spent his days working indoors.

His scent wafted toward her. A fresh and woodsy fragrance, along with an unmistakable beer or wine odor.

Her panic flared. It wasn't often that mortals, drunk or otherwise, happened upon this place. When they did, she had ironclad rules to follow. First, buzz Constance, her BFF who was also a voodoo priestess. Given Constance's power, she could remove memories by laying her hands on someone's head. A necessary evil so the mortal world would never know what went on within these walls. Following that, Heather was supposed to notify Becca, also her BFF, and a half-mortal witch who owned this place.

She leaned over her desk to press the intercom button.

The guy turned to her, blinked and stared.

His eyes were amazing, the color of Lipton tea, ringed by long, sooty lashes, his attention riveted as he drank her in. Given his slow, sexy smile, Heather suspected he undressed her with his eyes.

Her skin burned worse than it had when she'd faced Satan, yet this heat felt good, like comfort and excitement combined. She hadn't a clue why that would be and didn't have time to figure it out. She needed to get the others up here.

He groaned mournfully.

The agonized sound surprised her. Her empathetic nature kicked up several notches. "Are you all right?"

"Fuck, no," he panted. "These pissing boots are killing me."

They were as masculine as him, the tooled black leather sporting thick silver buckles. Although they weren't refined or gentlemanly, she liked them. Now, his language...

"I gotta sit down." He lurched to her desk.

"No. Please." She held out her hand to stop him. "Go back outside and —"

An ear-shattering howl ripped through the office. Roaring thunder followed. The were wailed away.

He stared at the hall and the treatment rooms beyond.

Too late now for him to waltz out of here with his memories intact. Heather felt bad about that but had to do the right thing for her friends and the service. "Let me get Constance."

His legs bowed. "I need to take a load off." He eyed her chair.

She raced toward him without thinking, desperate to block him from commandeering a seat. Her forehead barely reached his shoulder and he also outweighed her by ninety pounds or better, but she couldn't let him see anything on her computer screen. It would expose the business even more than the were's outburst had. If this guy left before Constance removed his memories... Heather didn't want to consider the possible exorcisms and purges that would follow.

The people who worked here were her family — the only real one she had. To protect them, she'd become more than assertive with him, she'd get rude, maybe even mean. She struggled to frown.

He staggered back to the door. Propped against it, he pulled off his right boot. It clunked on the faux-brick floor. His left boot followed.

Air hissed through his teeth.

Heather pressed her hand to her chest. She'd expected to see his socks, maybe even his bare feet, not hooves. "You're not mortal."

"No kidding." He puffed out another breath. "That's why I'm here." He gestured to the reception area stuffed with potted plants and feathery ferns. The greenery made the coral walls seem even warmer in comparison. Faux-gas fixtures provided a dated, romantic feel, like old New Orleans.

Loud hisses and teeth snapping filled the hall.

He arched one dark eyebrow and raked his gaze over her.

Perspiration rolled down her back and between her breasts.

Pleasure sparkled in his beautiful eyes. "I take it I'm in the right place for a makeover?"

Few beings had deeper voices than his. Awe blossomed within her. A pleasant feeling. Her nipples tightened. She liked that, too, when she shouldn't have. Given the huge bulge behind his fly, she guessed what he was. "You're a satyr, right?"

"That's me. Wine, women and song." He winked.

A zombie moaned.

He looked over. "Speaking of song, you should get a sound system in here. Drown out those crappy noises with some down-and-dirty heavy metal. You like Behemoth? Their *Lucifer* kicks serious ass."

His bulge got bigger, the folds between her legs damper. Fighting dizziness, Heather plodded to her computer, mystified as to why he had such an enticing effect on her when other guys had only sparked panic. Satyrs were charming, sure, and natural seducers. They had to be, considering all they thought about and wanted was sex. However, they didn't have the power to turn a good fairy against her ingrained principles. At least, she didn't think they could. "Do you have an appointment, Mister…"

"No Mister, just Daemon. Nope on the appointment, too. I'm hoping you can fit me in. What are you?"

Heather stopped keying. "The receptionist."

He laughed with pleasure, not derision.

The deep, virile sound rushed straight past her bones and into her marrow. Her belly fluttered.

"I mean what kind of being are you? No, wait. Let me guess." He tapped his forefinger against his bristly jaw.

He wore an ornate silver ring with a large black stone on his right middle finger. His hands were big and rugged rather than frightening.

Heather wasn't certain why, but she saw good strength in them, the sort that cherished and made mortal women sigh in appreciation.

She might have whimpered in delight, but didn't have enough breath.

He made a frustrated sound. "You're either an elf or a fairy. Damn, I can never tell those two beings apart."

That hurt deep. Fairies and elves weren't similar at all. No different from mistaking a satyr for a centaur. Despite his rude comment, she couldn't be surly or sarcastic. "I'm a good fairy."

Home of Erotic Romance

Sign up for our newsletter and find out about all our romance book releases, eBook sales and promotions, sneak peeks and FREE romance books!

About the Author

Tina is an Amazon and international bestselling novelist who writes passionate romance for every taste–'heat with heart'–for traditional publishers and indie. Booklist, Publisher's Weekly, Romantic Times and numerous online sites have praised her work. She's won Readers' Choice Awards, was named a finalist in the EPIC competition, received a Book of the Year award, The Golden Nib Award, awards of merit in the RWA Holt Medallion competitions, and second place in the NEC RWA contests. She's featured in the Novel & Short Story Writer's Market. Before penning romances, she worked at a major Hollywood production company in Story Direction.

Tina loves to hear from readers. You can find her contact information, website details and author profile page at https://www.totallybound.com